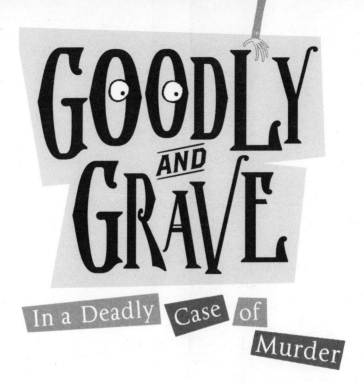

GOODLY AND GRAVE

In a Deadly Case of Murder

Books by Justine Windsor

GOODLY AND GRAVE IN A BAD CASE OF KIDNAP

GOODLY AND GRAVE IN A DEADLY CASE OF MURDER

GOODLY AND GRAVE

In a Deadly Case of Murder

JUSTINE WINDSOR

ILLUSTRATED BY BECKA MOOR

HarperCollins *Children's Books*

HarperCollins
PUBLISHERS
Since 1817

First published in Great Britain by
HarperCollins *Children's Books* in 2017
HarperCollins *Children's Books* is a division of HarperCollins*Publishers* Ltd,
HarperCollins Publishers
1 London Bridge Street
London SE1 9GF

The HarperCollins website address is:
www.harpercollins.co.uk

1

ISBN 978–0–00–818356–1

Typeset in Lido STF 12/18pt by Palimpsest Book Production Limited
Falkirk, Stirlingshire
Printed and bound by CPI Group (UK) Ltd, Croydon, CR0 4YY

For Charlie and Nikki

PROLOGUE

The graveyard was silent and deserted. An owl hooted from the great oak tree that grew next to the church. A fox slunk stealthily between the headstones, perhaps hunting for voles or on its way to raid the vicar's henhouse. When the church gate creaked open, the fox froze and listened intently, sniffing the night air. A man crept into view, carrying a lantern in one hand and a spade in the other. A large bag was slung over his shoulder. The

1

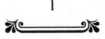

fox trotted silently away, melting into the dark of the moonless night. As for the man, he made his way over to two freshly dug graves. A cage of iron encased one of them and the man cursed softly under his breath when he saw it. But the other grave had no such protection. The man put his bag and his lantern down next to it, plunged his spade into the mound of soil and began to dig.

CHAPTER ONE

A GRAVE AFFAIR

"So this is where it all 'appens, Luce," Smell the cat said to Lucy Goodly, nodding towards a large wooden door.

Lucy took a deep breath, trying to control her nerves. She was about to attend her first official meeting of Magicians Against the Abuse of Magic, otherwise known as MAAM. It was a big moment for any magician, but an especially big moment for a

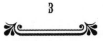

new magician like Lucy. A month ago she hadn't even known she was magical.

Lucy turned the handle, but the door wouldn't budge.

"Only opens when you say the password," Smell advised, gazing at Lucy. He was not the most attractive cat in the world, with his one and a half ears, stumpy tail and single eye.

"You could have said! What is it?"

"'avana."

The door stayed resolutely shut.

Smell made an impatient noise. "*H*avana," he said, putting a rather sarcastic emphasis on the 'h'. In response, the door swung open to reveal a very grand wood-panelled room with large stained-glass windows.

"Come along, you two! We're about to start!" said Lord Grave, who was sitting at the head of a vast polished table. He was the leader of MAAM, owner of Grave Hall and Lucy's employer (Lucy was officially the boot girl at Grave Hall). His panther Bathsheba was snoozing at his feet.

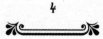

The other members of MAAM were gathered round the table. There was Lord Percy, a sorrowful-looking man with a deeply lined face. Sitting next to him was Lady Sibyl, a tall and elegant woman. Then there were the silver-haired twins, Beguildy Beguildy and Prudence Beguildy. Bertie Grave, Lord Grave's son, was also at the table. Bertie wasn't a magician and, in fact, didn't believe in magic (he thought magic could be explained by science), but he provided what he called "practical input" to MAAM.

Lucy hurriedly pulled out one of the heavy ornate chairs and sat down. Smell jumped on to her lap. There was so much to look at in this fascinating room and, being a very curious girl, Lucy wished there was time for her to explore everything thoroughly. She was especially intrigued by the enormous display cabinet that held numerous strange objects, some of which ticked and vibrated. Lucy guessed they were for magical crime-fighting purposes.

"Shall we begin?" Lord Grave said. "Now, I am sure you want to know why I've asked you all here. This is the reason."

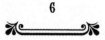

Lord Grave unfolded a newspaper and spread it out in the middle of the table. It was a copy of the *Penny Dreadful*. Lord Grave always called the *Penny* a "frightful old rag" but seemed to one of its most avid readers nonetheless.

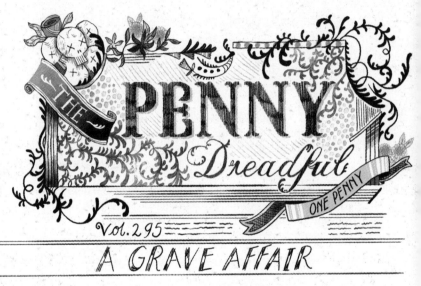

THE PENNY Dreadful

ONE PENNY

Vol. 295

A GRAVE AFFAIR

POLICE INVESTIGATIONS REACH A DEAD END

PROGRESS has stalled in the hunt for the graverobbers who have been targeting graves all over the country in the last few months. Dozens of relatives of the recently deceased have been left traumatised by the desecration of their loved ones' graves.

On page three, the respected scientist Sir Absalom Balderdash explains how the recent disappearances may be the work of flesh-eating zombies.

"Every robbery has coincided with the phase of the new moon. The new moon, also known as the dark moon, has always been associated with the supernatural and nefarious deeds. I am of the opinion that the evidence points to corpse-eating zombies."

Sir Absalom's theory is slightly flawed, however. The most puzzling aspect of this case is that the corpses are left untouched. It is only the soil covering the graves that is stolen.

"So, does anyone want to put forward a guess about what's behind these activities?" Lord Grave asked.

"It says here," said Prudence Beguildy, "that Sir Absalom Balderdash is convinced it's the work of corpse-eating zombies."

"A ridiculous man," her brother replied. "If anyone so much as picks a daffodil illegally, Sir Absalom blames it on zombies."

"Can I have some serious ideas, please?" snapped Lord Grave.

"It's graverobbers, of course!" Bertie said. His voice was somewhat hoarse as he had a bad cold. "It's rather unethical, but if medical science is to progress, we have to understand how the human body works."

"But look," Lucy said, pointing to one of the paragraphs in the article. "It's only the grave dirt that's stolen. Not the bodies."

"Oh, sorry," said Bertie, going rather red before sneezing violently into his handkerchief.

"Don't be sorry, my boy, all theories are welcome.

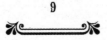

But Lucy is right," Lord Grave said. "That's why I think there may be a rogue magician at work. Strangely enough, the *Penny*'s advice on mortsafes is a good idea. Iron can impede magic."

"But why would a magician steal grave dirt?" Lucy asked.

"Why would a magician steal grave dirt?" said Beguildy Beguildy, who had been sitting with one elbow on the table, cheek resting on his hand and looking thoroughly bored all through the conversation. "Grave, I thought you said she was bright?"

"Don't be so mean, B," Prudence said.

"Quite," Lord Grave replied. "Lucy *is* bright as well as magically gifted. That's why I want her with me to begin an initial investigation into these thefts."

Lucy turned to Beguildy and flashed him a wide smile. He bared his teeth at her in a silent grimace.

"What you need to know, Lucy, and you, Bertie," Lord Grave continued, "is that grave dirt taken from freshly dug graves has powerful magical qualities."

Lucy looked at the article in the *Penny* again. "Is

all this about nefarious deeds and the new moon true?"

Lord Grave nodded. "For once it's not just the *Penny* being hysterical. The new moon *is* strongly associated with dark magic. Now, it seems the graverobber visited St Olaf's yesterday night, which is just a few villages away from here. The local gravedigger disturbed him before any grave dirt could be stolen. I suggest a surveillance operation."

"You think it's worth it, George?" Lady Sibyl said. "I doubt the robber will return."

"I think he might. Tonight's the last night of the new moon. There won't be another for a month and he may not have the time to seek out more newly dug graves to rob. He may chance his arm. And we can look for clues too." Lord Grave took out his pocket watch. "It's half past four. Sunset will be in about three hours. Lucy and I will go to St Olaf's and see if the graverobber makes another attempt. Does that suit you, Lucy?"

"Yes!" Lucy replied, almost leaping out of her seat with enthusiasm. Of course it suited her! She couldn't

wait to get stuck into her first official investigation for MAAM.

"Very well. Meet me in the grounds at half past six. Everyone, make no mention of this case outside these four walls for now."

Lord Grave then invited the members of MAAM into his drawing room for tea. Unfortunately, Lucy wasn't invited. To everyone not part of the magical world, Lucy was Lord Grave's boot girl, and her task was to keep all the shoes at the Hall spick and span. Becky Bone, the housemaid, would serve tea to all the guests, so it would look very odd for Lucy to be among them. Lucy had hoped that becoming part of MAAM might mean the end of her boot girl duties. But Lord Grave thought it best to maintain the pretence for now, especially because there was a reporter from the *Penny* called Slimeous Osburn, who took a marked interest in goings-on at Grave Hall and was often snooping around. If Osburn got wind of a Grave Hall servant suddenly being treated as a member of the household, he might become suspicious. So Lucy rather reluctantly left the rest of

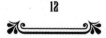

MAAM to it and headed off to the kitchen. As she passed Beguildy Beguildy, he made a rude face at her.

"Beware of the ghosties tonight!" he said, fluttering his hands at either side of his head. "Woo!"

Lucy held her head high and stalked away, but inwardly fantasised about emptying a brimming chamberpot over Beguildy's head. She smiled to herself as she imagined its stinky contents dripping down his face. As she set off down the stairs towards the kitchen, she sensed someone following her. It was Smell.

"Don't let that Beguildy get to you, Luce," he said, flicking his one and a half ears back and forth.

"I won't. But why is he so horrible to me?"

"Jealous."

Lucy stopped and looked down at Smell. "Jealous?"

Smell licked his front paw. "Yeah. See, Beguildy Beguildy's ambitious. Only been a member of MAAM for a few months, but fancies 'imself as a future 'ead. Now 'e thinks Grave's training you up to take his place one day."

"Me? That would be incredible," Lucy said, setting off again. The thought of Beguildy Beguildy being jealous of her because she might one day be head of MAAM was most pleasing and she firmly resolved to ignore any future taunts he might make. And anyway, she had more important things to think about. She was determined to be the one to crack the case of the grave-robbing magician.

CHAPTER TWO

THE COACHMAN AND THE STINKING BISHOP

As Lucy and Smell entered the kitchen, Smell grew silent. This was because Violet Worthington the scullery maid was there. Both Violet and Becky were completely unaware that Lord Grave, his friends and some of his servants were magicians and so any hint of magic had to be carefully hidden from them, especially something as remarkable as a talking cat.

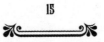

Lucy's own (non-magical) pet cat Phoebe was curled up under the kitchen table. Smell was terribly taken with her and as soon as he glimpsed her, he scooted over and attempted to touch noses, as cats sometimes do when they meet each other. Sadly, Phoebe was as unimpressed as ever with Smell's advances and very nearly took his one remaining eye out with her claws.

"Lucy, you're just in time for a pot of tea!" boomed Mrs Crawley, who was wearing her best flowery apron. Lucy had been rather confused by Mrs Crawley the first time she had met her as the bearded cook-cum-housekeeper was actually a man. But Lucy soon became used to the fact that Lord Grave insisted on the Grave Hall cook being addressed as Mrs regardless of gender or marital status – it was simply the done thing. Lucy was also used to Mrs Crawley's preference for frocks (*They keep the nether regions cool in a hot kitchen!* she often said). Lucy herself was unconventional in her clothing choices. Most girls wore dresses and curled their long hair. Lucy preferred to wear a jacket and breeches and wore her hair in a shining black bob.

"Take a seat, Lucy. You too, Violet, you deserve a break," Mrs Crawley said.

"Thanks, Mrs Crawley." Violet put down the huge copper pot she was scouring. Caruthers, Violet's small stuffed woollen frog, peeped out from her apron pocket. Wherever Violet went, Caruthers went too, which was something Becky Bone teased her mercilessly about. Thankfully, Becky was running some errands in Grave Village, which meant everyone could enjoy their cups of tea without having to look at her scowling face.

There was a third person in the kitchen, sitting at the table, a young man Lucy had never seen before. He gave her a friendly wink.

"Hello," she said uncertainly.

The man pushed his floppy black hair back from his forehead, and gazed at her very intently. Lucy felt herself blushing. The man smiled. "You're Miss Goodly, I take it? It's a pleasure to meet you."

"This is Mr Stephen Rivers," Mrs Crawley said.

"Oh, please, everyone just calls me Rivers!"

"He's Lady Sibyl's coachman," Mrs Crawley continued, bringing over the teapot while Violet set out the cups. Thankfully, the tea seemed to be the normal everyday variety. Mrs Crawley was prone to bouts of experimental cooking and had once served Lucy fried-egg-flavour tea.

"Under-coachman, actually," Rivers corrected. "But the head coachman has come down with a very nasty case of measles along with the rest of Lady Sibyl's household except for me, so I'm the main man for the moment. I must say I'm rather enjoying being in charge. And I only started working for her Ladyship a couple of months ago!"

As Lady Sibyl's coach was not an ordinary sort of coach (Lucy had seen it in action once; it was pulled by flying horses), Lucy guessed Rivers must be a magician. But of course she couldn't mention anything about this in front of Violet.

"Rivers is going to be with us for a few days, Lucy. Poor Lady Sibyl is very worried about catching measles herself so Lord Grave has invited her to stay until the danger is past. Would you like another slice of cake, Rivers?"

"No, thank you, Mrs Crawley. I must get on; the horses need grooming," Rivers said, getting to his feet. "I'll see you all later."

"He's a lovely man, isn't he?" Mrs Crawley said when Rivers had left. She stroked her beard thoughtfully. "I was thinking about making him a special welcome dinner. Edible dormouse with fried potatoes and sprouts stuffed with Stinking Bishop."

"Stuffed with a stinking bishop?" Lucy said in horror, imagining that Mrs Crawley had decided to widen her repertoire to include cannibalistic cookery.

"It's a type of cheese." Mrs Crawley chuckled, smoothing her apron. "And I thought I'd follow it with cockroach and cherry stargazey pie for dessert. What do you think?"

"It sounds delicious, but I won't be here I'm afraid," Lucy said, trying her best to sound disappointed. "I have to go out with Lord Grave and we might not be back until late."

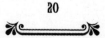

"Oh, not to worry. I'll save you some!" Mrs Crawley beamed.

"I'll look forward to it," Lucy said, hoping that she and Lord Grave would be back far too late to eat dinner. And, as it turned out, they very nearly didn't make it back at all.

✳

At half past six that evening, as arranged, Lucy met Lord Grave out in the grounds of Grave Hall. Because St Olaf's was a few villages away from Grave Hall, Lucy had expected that they would go in the carriage. However, Lord Grave ushered her to a quiet part of the pristine gardens, Bathsheba loping along by his side. As they picked their way across the grass, a splashing and trumpeting came from the direction of his Lordship's wildlife park. Lucy had been at the Hall long enough to know that this was the sound of the elephants taking their evening bath in the lake.

"Hold this for a moment please," Lord Grave said, handing the as yet unlit lantern he was carrying to Lucy. He dug around in his pocket and pulled out a

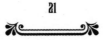

small illustrated pamphlet that he passed to Lucy, taking the lantern back off her. The pamphlet was for St Olaf's Church fete and had a drawing of the church on the front.

"This is St Olaf's, Lucy. Do you think you can manage it?"

"Manage what?"

"A shortcut, of course."

As part of her magical training with Lord Grave, Lucy had been practising shortcuts, a method of travelling that very few magicians were able to perform. Lucy had found out by accident that this was something she could do when she'd had to escape from a wicked magician called Amethyst Shade. Now Lord Grave was helping her learn to control this power.

"I think I'll be able to. Is Bathsheba coming too? Won't she be in the way a bit?"

"I'd prefer she came with us." Something in Lord Grave's tone suggested that he was secretly a little worried about what they might find at St Olaf's. This made Lucy a little worried too, but she tried not to

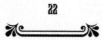

let nerves ruin her concentration as she thoroughly studied the picture of the church. Then she closed her eyes, fixed the image firmly in her mind and imagined herself there as strongly as she could.

"Excellent," Lord Grave said softly after a few moments.

Lucy opened her eyes. Sparks fizzled in the crisp evening air, signalling that magic was afoot. They began to join together, forming a slash, which widened into a hole. Lucy gave a quiet whoop of victory. She'd done it! St Olaf's Church and graveyard lay on the other side of the opening. Her very first official investigation of magical crime was about to begin.

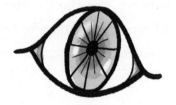

CHAPTER THREE

ANGEL EYES

Lord Grave and Bathsheba climbed through the opening, followed by Lucy. She always found it a strange sensation to grab the rubbery edges of a shortcut as she stepped through to the other side. When the three of them were standing safely in St Olaf's graveyard, Lucy reversed the shortcut by closing her eyes and this time imagining the opening growing smaller and smaller. Sure

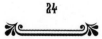

enough, when she reopened her eyes, the hole she'd made was shrinking rapidly to a pinpoint. There was a gust of wind, which ruffled Lucy's hair, followed by a loud sucking noise as the hole sealed itself shut.

"So what do we do next?"

"We need to speak to that gentleman over there," Lord Grave said. The gentleman in question was trimming the grass round the edges of the graveyard. Lord Grave strode over to him.

"Good evening, my man, are you Mr Brakespear?"

Mr Brakespear didn't reply. He was too busy staring goggle-eyed at Bathsheba.

"That's a . . . a . . ." he gibbered.

"Panther. Yes. Perfectly tame, I assure you. Could I ask a few questions about what happened here yesterday evening?"

"But I've already spoken to the parish constable!"

"Yes, of course. But we're detectives. Different area of expertise. Would you mind explaining again what happened?"

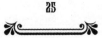

"C-certainly," Mr Brakespear replied, continuing to eye Bathsheba warily. "I had a busy day yesterday. I'd buried Mr Shannon and Mrs Munt in the afternoon. So I was down at the Bird in Hand having a quiet pint before going home to bed. Then one of the other regulars came in, said they'd seen light in the graveyard. So I thought I'd better have a look."

"Do go on," said Lord Grave.

"Someone was standing on Mr Shannon's grave over there, digging away." Mr Brakespear pointed to a fresh grave on the other side of the graveyard. "Couldn't tell if it was a man or a woman; they were too far away. I called out to warn 'em off. Soon as they heard my voice whoever it was scarpered. When I went to check I found that Mr Shannon's grave had a big hole in the soil. But the coffin hadn't been touched. Reckon I disturbed the thief before they could get to it. It's quite shook us all up. The vicar's going to get some more mortsafes in, like that one on Mrs Munt's grave. There's a good offer in the *Penny*—"

"Most disturbing," Lord Grave said. "Do you have any thoughts on what might be happening?"

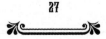

"Well, have you read the *Penny*? Sir Absalom—"

"Ah yes, I'm well versed in Sir Absalom's crackpot theories. Well, thank you for your help; we won't keep you any longer. Oh, just a second, there's a fly on your forehead." Lord Grave reached out and placed the tip of his right index finger between the gravedigger's eyebrows. Sparks crackled up the middle of his forehead, over his cap and down to the back of his head. Mr Brakespear's eyes grew wide and unfocused. After a few seconds, Lord Grave removed his finger. The gravedigger silently turned on his heel and walked off.

"Why did you do that?" Lucy asked. "And what was it?"

"I didn't want him remembering us, just in case. If he mentions anything to the parish constable about detectives making enquiries, it could raise awkward questions. So I tweaked him."

"You did what?"

"Tweaked him."

Suddenly Lucy realised what he meant. Lord Grave had tweaked the memories of the children she'd rescued from the clutches of Amethyst Shade to remove all traces of their ordeal from their minds. But until now, she'd never seen a tweak performed. It was most impressive how effortless he made it seem. She suspected it was harder than it looked.

"Can I learn how to tweak?"

"Yes, when I think you're ready. It's a very delicate skill you know. Multi-purpose too. You can tweak personalities as well as memories, for example. But get it wrong and you're in dire straits. Now, let's get on. We need something to hide behind, just in case my instincts are right and our graverobber makes a reappearance."

"Look, we could hide behind that," Lucy said, pointing to a statue of an angel, which stood near Mr Shannon's grave. The statue was somewhat disturbing to look at. It was green with lichen and had holes where its eyeballs should be. However, the handy thing about the angel was that it stood on a tall, wide plinth, which could screen Lucy and Lord Grave as well as Bathsheba while affording a decent view of Mr Shannon's grave.

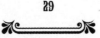

The sun began to set, accompanied by the twittering of the birds roosting in the trees. As darkness fell, the birds stopped singing one by one until a robin perched on the roof of the church gave the very final chirrup of the day. After that, the sounds of the night began. Bushes rustled with unseen creatures. An owl swooped overhead before diving towards the ground. There was a high-pitched squeak, and the owl arced back into the sky, a struggling mouse clutched in its talons.

The temperature in the churchyard was rapidly dropping. Lucy shivered a little and thought longingly of the cosy kitchen at Grave Hall. Mrs Crawley often made hot milk for everyone at the end of the day, sweetened with honey from the bees that Vonk the butler looked after.

"How long do you think we should stay for?" she asked Lord Grave.

"Until sun-up if need be. Now shush, we need to keep as quiet as possible."

A moment later, Lord Grave sneezed loudly.

"That's not exactly keeping quiet, is it?" Lucy whispered.

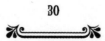

"I think I've caught Bertie's cold," Lord Grave said stiffly. "Luckily, I planned ahead." He took a small bottle from his pocket, which contained a luminous yellow liquid. He unscrewed the top and drank the contents, his whole face and even his moustache twisting in disgust. Seconds later, steam piped out of his ears, wreathing himself, Lucy, Bathsheba and the angel in luminous yellow mist.

"What is that?" Lucy whispered.

"A cold remedy. Mrs Crawley gave it to me. You know, I think it's working!"

Thankfully, the remedy did indeed seem to work, as there was no more sneezing or coughing from Lord Grave over the course of the next two hours, by which time Lucy was on the brink of screaming with boredom. Just when she thought she couldn't bear it a moment longer, Lord Grave nudged her.

"Someone's coming," he said in a low voice.

Lucy peered round the side of the eyeless angel's plinth. Sure enough, a tall man was approaching, carrying a lantern. It was impossible to see his face properly as he had a scarf wrapped round his nose and mouth and the light from the lantern cast a shadow across his eyes and forehead. He carried a spade.

"Let's wait a few moments. See what he does," Lord Grave whispered.

They watched as the man reached Mr Shannon's grave. He set his lantern down and began shovelling grave dirt into the bag he had with him.

"Oh no!" Lord Grave exclaimed softly.

"What is it?" Lucy whispered back.

"The dratted cold remedy's wearing off. I'm going to . . . going to . . ."

Lucy hesitated, wondering whether she should put her hand over Lord Grave's nose and mouth. He might think such an action very insubordinate. But before she could decide, his Lordship let rip a violent cough combined with a ferocious sneeze. The cough and the sneeze echoed around the graveyard, waking up the sleeping birds, which chirped and chattered in alarm.

Lucy held her breath, hoping that by some miracle the man hadn't heard the commotion. But of course

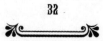

he had and he swiftly picked up the half-filled bag of grave dirt and sprinted off, something falling as he ran.

As soon as the man was out of sight, Lucy and Lord Grave leaped out from behind the stone angel. Lord Grave lit the lantern they had brought with them so they could investigate the object the man had dropped.

"It's some sort of book," Lucy said, bending down to pick it up, but before she could do so Lord Grave grabbed her arm.

"Wait. In this business, Lucy, it's vital to assume everything is dangerous until you've proved otherwise."

Lucy could see his point. She had made the disastrous mistake of trusting magical objects before, namely a clockwork raven, which had turned out to be a wicked magician in disguise. "So how do we tell whether it's safe to touch?"

Lord Grave took what looked like a fat silver pencil from his pocket. "This is one of Lord Percy's contraptions. It whistles if it detects harmful magic

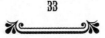

in an object. It's Percy's strongest skill, you know, to—"

A grating noise interrupted Lord Grave. Bathsheba gave a low growl of warning. Before Lucy could turn to see where the noise was coming from, a great stone fist slammed down on Lord Grave's head, flattening his top hat and sending him slumping to the ground. The plinth the eyeless angel had stood on moments before was now empty. Its former occupant stepped over Lord Grave's prone body and lunged at Lucy, growling in a completely un-angelic manner.

CHAPTER FOUR

THE NOT SO PITILESS PREDATOR

B
athsheba roared ferociously at the angel and leaped at it, her fangs and claws bared, but even these powerful weapons couldn't damage stone. The angel shook the panther off like an irritating fly before grabbing Lucy by the collar and hauling her up until the two of them were face to face. Those awful empty eyes stared into Lucy's and the stone lips curled into a snarl. Lucy wriggled and squirmed. The angel's grip was slowly choking her.

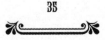

The angel began clomping heavily through the grass towards the grave that had been disturbed. The robber had returned and was bending down to pick up the book he had dropped.

"Bathsheba," Lucy managed to choke out, "attack that man – please attack!"

The panther seemed to understand Lucy's command. She hunkered down into a crouch before launching herself at the graverobber, knocking him over. The book he'd retrieved moments before left his grasp again. This time, it flew from his hand and landed in the tangle of a nearby overgrown grave. The man had no chance to run after it: Bathsheba had pinned him to the ground in an instant.

With the man safely pinioned and the precious clue secure for now, Lucy turned her attention to escaping her stony captor's clutches. As a first stab at gaining her freedom, Lucy poked the angel in its empty eyehole, but this made no impact whatsoever. Panic swamped Lucy as she struggled and choked in the angel's grasp. The angel twisted the collar of her jacket so that it dug painfully into her windpipe. If

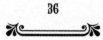

she didn't escape soon she was going die of strangulation! Anger began to overtake Lucy's panic and fear. She wasn't going to let this happen to her.

"Why are you doing this?" Lucy spluttered out between choking coughs. "You're supposed to be on . . . be on . . . the side of good. Which is my side! Put me down."

The angel's grip on Lucy's collar loosened. Lucy took in great ragged gulps of air. Her captor stared at her. A dim light glimmered in its eyeholes as though Lucy's admonishments had sparked life in there. But the light died after a few seconds and the angel's grip tightened again. Lucy frantically tried to fathom what was happening. Was getting angry with the angel triggering some kind of magic? Although Lucy's magical abilities were still very new to her and she didn't understand much about how it all worked, she did know that imagining what you wanted to happen sometimes played a part. Lucy held on to her anger, refusing to let fear take over.

"You ... should be ... ashamed of yourself, helping a criminal!" she said between gasps for air.

Again the angel's eyes glinted. Again it paused in its efforts to strangle Lucy. Convinced now that her anger was having an effect, Lucy continued to berate her attacker. At the same time, she visualised the angel releasing her and pursuing the graverobber instead. As deeply and vividly as she could, she imagined landing on the soft grass, the ground vibrating as the stone angel pounded towards the graverobber, and his cries as the angel imprisoned him in her stony arms. She held the images in her mind.

And held them there.

And held them there.

The grip on Lucy's collar loosened, sending her tumbling to the grass. She rolled out of the way of the angel's feet; it was clumping towards the graverobber now, just as she'd imagined it doing. With the angel suitably distracted, Lucy crawled swiftly over to Lord Grave, who was still lying flat out on the grass. She shook him.

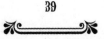

"Sir, sir, please wake up!"

But Lord Grave lay frighteningly still. Lucy put her ear against his chest. She could just about make out the comforting *whump whump* of his heart. She sat back on her heels, shaky with relief that at least Lord Grave wasn't dead. But now she needed to get help and fast! The best thing to do was to shortcut back to Grave Hall and fetch help. She briefly surveyed the situation. The angel was looming over the graverobber now, and Bathsheba still had him firmly under her paws, so hopefully there was no immediate danger.

Lucy hurriedly began the process of shortcutting back to Grave Hall, imagining herself in the meeting room where the rest of MAAM would be waiting. But before she'd got very far, a rough but friendly tongue licked the back of her neck.

"Bathsheba! You're supposed to be guarding the . . ." She looked frantically around and saw that the graverobber was now free and on his feet, seeking the book he'd dropped. Even worse, the angel had turned away from and was heading for Lucy again, its face contorted with anger.

"Go back to him, girl. Get him!" Lucy cried to Bathsheba.

Bathsheba turned and bounded off towards the man again. But instead of attacking him, she flopped down at his feet and rolled over on her back. The man paused in his search and scratched Bathsheba's belly as though she was a fluffy kitten and not a potentially lethal panther. He then continued his hunt, leaving Bathsheba sprawled contentedly on the grass.

Realising Bathsheba was a lost cause, Lucy turned her attention to the angel. It was almost upon her once more, looking as though it had some serious avenging in mind.

"I thought you'd changed sides!" Lucy yelled in frustration. She gathered all the mental energy she had left and pictured the angel turning round yet again and going after the graverobber. To her joy, after a few seconds, the angel did indeed change direction and began stomping back towards the

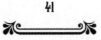

graverobber, who cried out angrily when he realised what was happening. This time, Lucy didn't let anything distract her thoughts. *She* was controlling the angel now and wouldn't let this man get the better of her! Concentrating harder and harder, she pictured the angel attacking the graverobber. Sure enough, the angel made a swipe at the man, he ducked just in time to narrowly miss a skull-cracking blow from the stone fist. He then decided that discretion was the better part of valour and took off in the opposite direction.

As Lucy watched him vanish into the night, her concentration wavered. The angel clumped along for a few more steps before coming to a stop. Lucy sagged to the ground in relief. A few moments later, Bathsheba came trotting back over and licked her face.

"A lot of help you were. You're supposed to be a pitiless predator not a lap cat!" Lucy said crossly. But she hugged the panther just the same. Then, to Lucy's very great relief, Lord Grave began to stir. She helped him sit up.

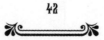

"What's that statue doing over there? Did it bash me over the head? I can't quite remember."

Lucy quickly explained what had happened and how she and the graverobber had battled for control of the angel.

"You *animated* it?"

"I don't know what that means."

"It means that you made an inanimate object come to life. It's a very rare skill."

Lucy wanted to ask more about animation, but this wasn't the time. Lord Grave had turned as grey as the stone angel. "We should get back to the Hall, sir. You look terrible."

Lord Grave ignored her concern. "We need to retrieve that book. It's an important clue," he said, his voice beginning to sound worryingly slurred.

Lucy snatched up the lantern, which luckily hadn't gone out. "You stay here. I'll find it. I think I know roughly where it landed." Lord Grave didn't argue, much to Lucy's surprise. That surprise became apprehension when she realised he had dozed off.

"Stay with him, Bathsheba, I'll be as quick as I

can." She hurried off, scared that Lord Grave's injuries were more serious than she'd first thought and that he might die before she found the book and got them all back to Grave Hall.

CHAPTER FIVE

THE SNAKE OUROBOROS

L ucy's fears were unfounded, however, and a couple of hours later, she was safely back at Grave Hall and sitting with Lord Percy and Lady Sibyl at the table in the MAAM meeting room. She had managed to retrieve the graverobber's book after a few minutes of searching and then opened a shortcut back to Grave Hall where Bertie, Lord Percy and Lady Sibyl had been anxiously waiting. They'd helped Lord Grave, who was semi-conscious again,

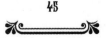

through the shortcut. Mrs Crawley had then carried him up to bed.

Smell was on the table, padding around and sniffing at the book. Lucy had been surprised to find it was simply a blank notebook. She had been expecting it to contain spells or something of the sort. However, the cover was intriguing. It had been damp and muddy when she found it, but Lady Sibyl had carefully cleaned and dried it and now the tiny jewels embedded in its green leather cover gleamed.

The meeting-room door crashed open, making everyone jump. For one wild moment, Lucy expected the murderous angel to burst inside. But instead, the Beguildy twins rushed in.

"Where have you two been?" Lord Percy snapped. "We've had a real emergency here."

"We decided to have dinner with friends. Lady Sibyl's coachman flew us back as soon as we heard. Is Lord Grave all right? Where is he?" Prudence said breathlessly. The small ship she wore in her piled-up silvery hair had tilted sideways and her cloak was hanging half off one shoulder.

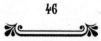

"Don't worry, Prue," Lady Sibyl said, patting Prudence's arm. "He's safe in bed at the moment, with a rather large bandage round his head. Young Bertie's with him; the boy won't let him out of his sight."

"What happened exactly? Did you make a hash of it, Lucy?" Beguildy asked.

"She couldn't have made less of a hash of it. Lucy saved Lord Grave's life and her own," Lord Percy said sternly. "I'll explain later. Come and look at this."

Beguildy looked decidedly pouty as he and Prudence joined everyone else at the table, where Smell was still meandering around the notebook, stopping every now and then to gingerly sniff at it.

"If only my detector hadn't been broken." Lord Percy sighed regretfully. The silver pencil-like detector had been smashed to pieces when the angel attacked Lord Grave.

"I don't need no detector, not with my nose," Smell replied. "This thing reeks of magic. But not a type of magic I've smelled before."

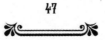

"What does this mean? Does anyone know?" Prudence asked, pointing to the symbol that decorated the edges of the notebook's pages in a repeating pattern. It was a snake holding its tail in its mouth.

"The snake ouroboros," Lord Percy said thoughtfully. "An ancient symbol in alchemy. It can mean a number of things: infinity, creation, destruction."

Before anyone could ask any questions about the snake ouroboros, the door opened once again. This time, Lord Grave wobbled into the room. He was dressed in his nightshirt, dressing gown and slippers and had a large bandage wrapped round his head. Bertie was hovering anxiously behind him.

Prudence rushed forward to help Lord Grave. He resisted at first, but then leaned on her arm and tottered over to the table where the notebook lay open.

"You should be in bed, Lord Grave!" Prudence said.

"That's what I told him!" Bertie agreed.

"Too much to do," Lord Grave said, half falling into the chair that Lord Percy had hastily pulled out for him. "Lucy. Are you all right? You look exhausted."

"I'm fine," Lucy said, although in truth she was feeling horribly tired now and was finding it hard to concentrate.

"Now, has anyone any ideas about this notebook?"

Prudence began fussing around Lord Grave. "Your bandage is coming loose, let me just—"

"Prudence!" Lord Grave said a little snappily. Then more gently, he added, "I appreciate the concern, Prue, my dear. But there's no need for it. I'm perfectly well."

Prudence looked rather upset. As she dejectedly sat down next to her brother, her gaze met Lucy's and they exchanged sympathetic smiles, although Prudence's was slightly tremulous round the edges.

"Smell is certain that the notebook has magical properties," Lord Percy said. "But we haven't progressed any further than that."

Lord Grave rubbed his forehead wearily, as though his head ached. Which was quite possible given he

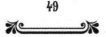

had recently been clonked over the head by a stone fist. "I think we should call in Angus Reedy."

"Good idea," Lord Percy said. "An experienced bookbinder like him should be able to give us some insight. I could send him one of my chits?"

"Yes, thank you. I believe he's on his way back from France, but the chit should still find him."

Lucy was very curious to find out what a chit was, so she watched carefully as Lord Percy went over to a writing bureau that stood against the wall next to the window. He opened it, took out a sheet of paper from one of the numerous drawers inside, and wrote a message on it, before rolling it up. He then carried it over to the window, which he unfastened. He placed the tube of paper in the palm of his hand and spoke to it. "Angus Reedy. Believed to be travelling back to England from France."

There was a buzzing noise. The paper trembled and sprouted two tiny wings. It flew out of Lord Percy's hand and buzzed off out of the window.

"That's amazing!" Lucy said. Although she was

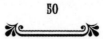

becoming more and more used to seeing magic now, much of it still surprised and delighted her.

"Another of Lord Percy's clever contraptions," Lady Sibyl said, looking fondly at him.

"It really is excellent," Lucy said to Lord Percy, whose face creased into a rare smile.

"I suppose there's not much more to be done tonight," Lord Grave said, bracing his hands against the arms of his chair and easing himself upright. "I suggest we all get some sleep."

✳

Lucy made her way to bed, feeling more exhausted than ever. Her bedroom, which she shared with Becky Bone, was high under the eaves at the front of Grave Hall. Lucy didn't like sharing a room with Becky, who could be grumpy and unpleasant, but she loved the view her from bedroom window as she could see out over to Grave Hall's wildlife park. She could have happily spent hours watching the animals. There were so many fascinating creatures roaming around.

Elephants (Lucy once had an unfortunate run-in with one of them), giraffes (ditto), lions, zebras and numerous other animals, as well as an abundance of birds. And Bathsheba was there too at times, of course. Although the panther spent her days padding around after Lord Grave, at night she slept in her hut in the wildlife park, because she had a regrettable habit of raiding the kitchen when everyone was asleep.

Lucy always liked to have a last look out of the window each evening before going to bed. Treading carefully so as not to wake Becky, who would give Lucy a bad-tempered earful if woken, she went to the window and opened the curtains a little. Under the bright stars, the wildlife park was calm and still apart from the shadowy outline of one of the giraffes strolling along. Bertie had informed her that giraffes only slept in short bursts because they had to get up frequently to keep their circulation moving.

Eventually Lucy yawned and closed the curtains. She changed into her nightgown and slipped into bed. Narrowly escaping death at the hands of a stone

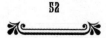

angel really was a tiring business and she was looking forward to having a good rest.

It seemed as though she'd only been sleeping for a few minutes when the screaming woke her.

CHAPTER SIX

THE BREAK-IN

L ucy leaped out of bed and stood shivering in the dark. Something banged in the house below.

"Did you hear that, Goodly?" Becky asked, sounding frightened. Lucy could see the housemaid's shadowy form sitting up in bed.

"Y-yes."

Usually Becky would have made a nasty comment about Lucy's shaky reply as she never missed a chance to be horrid. But fear seemed to be bringing

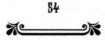

out her best side as she simply said, "We need some light."

There was the scrape of a match and welcome candlelight began to flicker and glow. United for once, Lucy and Becky hurried out into the hallway. Mrs Crawley was already there, carrying a candle. She was wearing a pair of unlaced boots and had flung a coat over her beribboned nightdress, but her beard was still in the three plaits she always wore it in for bed. She looked unusually stern.

"You girls stay here," she said as she headed towards the stairs. "I mean it, Lucy!"

Mrs Crawley clattered off, almost tripping over her bootlaces in her haste. Lucy waited for around a minute before setting off after her with Becky in tow. They followed the sound of voices and commotion, which led them to the bottom of the house and the entrance hall.

The whole household had gathered there. The enormous front door stood open. A huge hole had been gouged out where the lock had once been and the lion's-head knocker had a dent in it. Vonk, the

butler, was sitting on the tiled floor, a blood-soaked handkerchief held to his head.

"Oh," Becky whispered. "Look at Vonk. All that . . . all that . . . I think I'm going to . . ." She slumped to the floor. Nobody noticed apart from Lucy, who quickly bent over Becky to make sure the housemaid had simply fainted. Lucy knew she should really attract the attention of one of the grown-ups, but she wanted to take the chance to have a closer look at what was going on. Becky would come round on her own soon enough with no harm done.

She moved closer to the knot of Grave Hall residents and guests. Mrs Crawley was helping Vonk to his feet.

Lord Grave was there too. He was very shaky still from his own injuries and was having to be steadied by Bertie. Lady Sibyl and Lord Percy were carefully inspecting the damage to the front door. Lucy spotted Smell, nipping between people's legs and sniffing around. He trotted over to her, casting a cautious look at Becky.

"It's all right; she's only fainted."

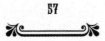

"That your doing, Luce? I know you don't like 'er, but—"

"No! I think it was the blood that set her off. What's happened to Vonk?"

"Tussle with a burglar. Don't know 'ow they managed it; that door is as strong as they come. Vonk was 'aving 'is bedtime cocoa in the butler's pantry. 'E 'eard a kerfuffle. Someone was out 'ere, about to take off with that notebook you found."

Lucy gasped. "It's been stolen? Oh, but it was our only clue!"

"What's been stolen?"

The sleepy voice behind Lucy made her flinch in surprise. She wasn't the only one to be startled. Being a cat, Smell's reflexes were much sharper than Lucy's and he leaped several metres into the air, his back arched.

"What you doing, creeping up on people like that?" he said irritably as he landed neatly back down on the tiled floor.

Rivers yawned. "Sorry. But what's going on?"

"I was just explaining to Lucy 'ere. There'd been

a break-in. Someone tried to nick –" Smell paused, blinking up at Rivers – "that painting hanging over the fireplace. But Vonk challenged 'im. There was a bit of a fight. Vonk's got a nasty cut and maybe a busted rib."

"Poor Vonk. I hope he'll be all right."

Everyone was bustling towards the stairs now and as Becky was beginning to stir Smell lapsed into silence. Mrs Crawley flashed a stern look at Lucy as she passed by, carrying a protesting Vonk in her arms.

"I can manage the stairs on my own, Mrs C! There's no need for this."

"Come on, Vonk, be sensible. You're in no fit state to be climbing great flights of stairs. It'll be bed rest for you for a few days."

"She's right, Vonk," Lord Grave said wearily as Bertie helped him up the stairs too. Becky was on her feet now as well.

"No need to help me up or anything, Goodly. I'm going back to bed," she snapped before tottering off.

Rivers yawned again. "I'll be off as well. You take care, Miss Goodly."

When Rivers and Becky were both out of earshot, Lucy turned to Smell. "Why did you lie about what the burglar tried to steal?"

"Thought it best not to say anything about the notebook. Lord Grave did say 'e wanted to keep the investigation quiet for now. You should get off to bed yourself, Luce. It'll be sun-up in a couple of hours."

"I'm going to take a look around first."

"Lord Percy and Lady Sib 'ave already done that. No clues to be found."

"I'd like to anyway."

Lord Grave had ordered that the lamps in the hallway should be kept burning until dawn as a precaution, so she would have plenty of light to see by.

Smell swished his tail and half closed his eye thoughtfully. "I'll stick around. Don't think you should be here alone."

With Smell trotting at her heels, Lucy began her investigations with the front door. Although the locks had been destroyed, the bolts on the inside were still intact and Lord Percy had refastened them. They were very stiff and heavy and Lucy struggled to undo them. Once she had managed it, she examined both sides of the door

"I reckon they used an axe to smash the lock in," Smell told her.

When Lucy tried to shut the door, she had some difficulty because of the strong wind that had picked up outside, blowing bits of twig and other debris into the house. Once the door was finally bolted again, she turned her attention to the rest of the entrance hall. Apart from a broken vase, which had been knocked from the hall table during the struggle between Vonk and the burglar, everything looked as it always did. The wood-panelled walls gleamed, the grandfather clock ticked soothingly, even the paintings on the walls remained hanging perfectly straight.

Lucy was about to give up and go to her room when she noticed a tiny movement on the floor as something drifted along in one of the many draughts that blew though the house. At first she thought it was just dust or fluff (one of Lucy's duties was to

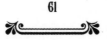

sweep the entrance hall, but she never made a very good job of it). When she looked more closely, she saw that it looked more like the remains of a broken spider's web, but a spider's web strung with tiny multi-coloured drops of rain.

"Smell, look at this!"

Smell padded over to her side. "Can't see nothing!"

"There! That webby thing!" She pointed, but Smell still couldn't see it. Lucy watched whatever it was twist and turn in the draught. After a moment or two, she bent down to take a closer look. Then she lightly touched it with her fingertip. The web erupted into a shower of sparks and vanished so quickly she wasn't sure what it was she had really seen.

CHAPTER SEVEN

COCKROACH CRUNCH

"It's very scary. I hope Lord Grave and Vonk get better soon," Violet said a few hours later, when the servants were in the kitchen having their elevenses. Of course, Violet and Becky had no idea that Lord Grave's head wound had been caused by a violent encounter with a stone angel; they both thought he'd been hurt during the attempted robbery along with Vonk.

"What about me?" Becky said. "I was out cold

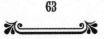

for hours from the shock of it all. I still don't feel right."

"I'm glad I wasn't here when it happened. They might have stolen Caruthers!" Violet clutched the knitted frog to her chest.

Becky opened her mouth, no doubt to make some scathing comment, but Rivers spoke over her.

"I think Caruthers is safe, Miss Worthington," he said. "We'll all be on our guard from now on."

"That's right, Violet," Mrs Crawley said reassuringly. "Now, Rivers, would you like another of my special crunch biscuits?"

Rivers held up his plate "No need to ask me twice, Mrs Crawley!"

Everyone else refused the offer and Lucy had to wonder whether Rivers knew that the special crunch element of the biscuits he was enthusiastically munching was, in fact, baked cockroach.

When elevenses had finished, everyone began to drift back to their various chores, leaving Lucy and Mrs Crawley alone in the kitchen. Lucy itched with impatience. She wandered around, picking things up and putting them down again. Lord Grave was still asleep and being jealously guarded by Bertie, but she was sure that he'd call a MAAM meeting once he was awake.

"Lucy! If you're at a loose end, you could be cleaning out Bathsheba's hut," Mrs Crawley said.

She was standing at the kitchen table, kneading a small piece of dough that would later miraculously become enough bread to feed the whole household. Once, Lucy would have wondered why such a small amount of food was being provided for everyone, but now she knew that Mrs Crawley had a very special skill and was able to make a small amount of food go an unexpectedly long way.

"What if Lord Grave wakes up and calls a meeting while I'm not here?"

"Someone will come and fetch you."

Lucy sighed, but went off to put her armour on. The armour was necessary to protect Lucy as she had to go inside the Grave Hall wildlife park to muck out Bathsheba's living quarters. Although Lucy knew Bathsheba well enough now not to be afraid of her (and the panther was with Lord Grave at the moment, as she'd refused to leave his side since last night) there were still lions and other potentially dangerous animals to contend with.

As she raked up Bathsheba's dirty straw, Lucy mulled over what had happened so far. Someone was stealing grave dirt for nefarious purposes. There was possibly a magical notebook involved in those nefarious purposes, but no one knew exactly how. It was almost certain that the same man who was robbing the graves had tried to steal the notebook back last night. Lucy wondered again about the silvery web she had noticed at the scene of the break-in. What could it have been? Perhaps some sort of magical residue? But the attacker hadn't used magic to break in and try to steal the notebook, just simple brute force. It was all so confusing and frustrating!

Lucy was considering all this as she pushed the wheelbarrow full of Bathsheba's used bedding back to the house when she saw Rivers hurrying towards her. She raised the visor of her helmet.

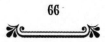

"Is everything all right?" she asked, suddenly afraid that something had happened to Lord Grave.

"Nothing to worry about at all. Lord Grave's awake and called a meeting of MAAM to discuss last night's break-in. Young Bertie's most annoyed, but his Lordship insisted. Here, let me take that wheelbarrow for you."

"Thanks," Lucy said, taking off her helmet.

"It's all very mysterious, isn't it, Miss Goodly?" Rivers said.

"What is?" Lucy replied cautiously, remembering what Smell had said about keeping the investigation quiet.

Rivers chuckled. "No need to be evasive. I had a meeting with Vonk this morning. I'm going to cover all his duties until he recovers. So of course he had to fill me in on everything that's been going on. Graverobbers and magical books! I must admit I envy you, Miss Goodly. I'm sure it's terribly exciting to be involved in MAAM!"

"It *is* exciting," Lucy agreed.

The wheels on the barrow squeaked as Rivers

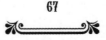

pushed it along. "How did you come to be involved, if you don't mind me asking?"

"It's a bit of a long story, but Lord Grave discovered me using magic to win poker games. I didn't even know I was doing magic! So he brought me here so he could train me to use magic properly."

"Do you have any family?"

"Yes, my parents."

"Don't they miss you? Don't you miss them?"

"Yes," Lucy admitted. She worried about them too, especially about her father who had a bad leg. She explained to Rivers that Lord Grave had made an agreement with her mother and father that she could stay at Grave Hall. Of course, Mr and Mrs Goodly thought that this was because she was an excellent boot girl and not because Lord Grave was training her to be a magician. To keep her parents out of trouble (they were hopeless without Lucy to look after them) Lord Grave had cast a good luck charm on them to make sure they won all their poker games, telling them he was sure Lady Luck would be good to them. This was partly so that they could earn

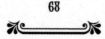

enough money to rebuild Leafy Ridge, the Goodly family home, which had burned down when her parents accidentally left a pigeon pie in the oven when they went off to play bridge.

"And *is* Lady Luck being good to them?" Rivers asked.

"I think so. I had a letter from them. They seem to be fine. They've gone to Venice. There's a famous casino there that they've always wanted to visit."

"Ah, yes. I've heard of it. The famous Casino di Venezia."

By now, Lucy and Rivers had reached the house. "Why don't you run along to your meeting, Miss Goodly? I'll get rid of this straw. It does whiff a bit, doesn't it?" Rivers said, wrinkling his nose.

✳

Once Lucy had changed out of her armour and into her usual clothes, she rushed off to the meeting room. Everyone else was already there, looking rather baggy-eyed from lack of sleep. Smell was stretched out on a sheaf of papers, snoring softly. Lucy slipped into her seat beside Bertie, who had a rather mutinous expression on his face. Lord Grave must have come straight from his bed as he was still in his night things. Bathsheba was there too, padding around the room uneasily as though she was as worried as Bertie about her master.

There was a knock on the door and Mrs Crawley came in, carrying Vonk in her beefy arms. He was wan and pale and swaddled in tight bandages from waist to chest. Even though Mrs Crawley set him down gently in one of the chairs, he winced in pain.

"I'm sorry to have to question you while you're so unwell and should be resting," Lord Grave told Vonk.

"He's not the only one who should be resting!" Bertie said.

Lord Grave looked at Bertie affectionately. "I promise you I'll go back to bed as soon as we're finished here. Now, Vonk, can you take us through what happened?"

Vonk explained what Lucy already knew: that he'd been having a bedtime cup of cocoa in his butler's pantry when he'd heard suspicious noises.

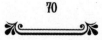

"I came out into the entrance hall and saw a man at the bottom of the stairs. He had the notebook under his arm. I shouted at him and he ran for the door. So I tackled him."

Lucy thought this was very brave of Vonk. He was an unusually small man, smaller than Lucy herself, in fact.

"What did this chap look like?" Lady Sibyl asked.

"He had a scarf over his face so I couldn't see. I tried to pull it off him, but he was too strong for me. But I did manage grab the notebook – he dropped it while we were fighting. When the vase fell off the table and broke, he must have realised that the noise would rouse the house, so he gave up and ran off."

"Do we know if he was on a horse or on foot?" Beguildy Beguildy said.

"On foot I think. I would have heard hooves on the gravel outside if he'd had a horse."

"Could he have used magic to escape?" Lucy said. She explained about the strange web-like thing she'd seen after the break-in. "I'm sure it was something

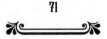

magical; could it have had anything to do with how he got away?"

Nobody replied. They were all too busy staring at Lucy, as though she'd said something very shocking indeed.

CHAPTER EIGHT

UNCLE EBENEZER'S QUILL

Lord Grave's eyebrows were nearly meeting his hair. Even Smell had half opened his eye.

"What, what is it? What have I said?"

Lord Grave's eyebrows lowered a little. "What you saw was a trace of magic. Traces are a mysterious phenomena. Very few magicians can see them and we know very little about them. But it's thought that whenever magic is performed, a remnant of energy is left behind, which is visible to some magicians."

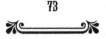

By now, Bertie had stopped looking and was listening intently. "Fingerprints!"

"What's that my boy?" Lord Grave said.

Bertie waggled his fingers in the air. "There's a surgeon, Mr Overton, who says that we all have our own unique fingerprints and that they could be used to solve crimes. Are these traces like that?"

Lord Grave nodded. "It's possible. Some people think traces are unique to each magician, but that's just one theory about them."

Bertie leaned forward. "So if Lucy saw this trace, can't we find a way of identifying who it belongs to?"

"Afraid not, my boy. As I said, it's just a theory."

Bertie sank back in his chair and crossed his arms again. "Someone should test that theory then. Now I know how Mr Overton feels. No one listens to him either."

As there was very little else to discuss for now, the meeting broke up. Lucy was about to leave with the others, when Lord Grave asked her to stay behind, much to Bertie's annoyance.

Once they were alone, Lord Grave motioned to the

sofas that were grouped around the enormous stone fireplace. When they had both settled themselves, Lord Grave took a cigar out of his dressing-gown breast pocket and lit it.

"Don't tell Bertie, he wants me to give up," he said as he took a puff, sighing in satisfaction. "Now as we have a moment of calm, can you explain to me exactly what it was you did in the graveyard? How did you control the angel?"

Lucy stared into the fire for a few moments, trying to put her strange experience into words.

"I was angry and frightened. I thought you might be dead, that I might be next. It all welled up in me."

Lord Grave nodded. "Sometimes intense emotions enable us to perform magic we didn't know we had in us. What happened next?"

"I told the angel it should be helping us not the graverobber. It stopped trying to hurt me as if it was obeying me for a few seconds. And so I thought I'd try telling it what to do next and imagine it at the same time. It worked and the angel let me go. But the graverobber was still half controlling it too. It was like a mental battle, both of us trying to control the angel, but somehow I won."

"Lucy, what you did was an incredible piece of magic. As I said to you last night, animation is a rare skill."

"Can you animate things?"

"Not really. It's something I never mastered. The only thing I have ever managed to partially animate is the statue of my great-grandmother."

"The one outside the Room of Curiosities?"

"That's right."

Lucy thought back to the time she had tickled the statue of Lord Grave's great-grandmother under the chin to make her come alive and hand over the keys to the Room of Curiosities, where she had got into all sorts of trouble. Had she been able to do that because of her animation skills?

Now it was Lord Grave's turn to stare thoughtfully into the fire. After a few moments, he said, "If you feel up to it, I'd like you to try animating something. Let's see . . . ah, Uncle Ebenezer."

"Who?"

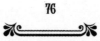

Lord Grave pointed to the portrait of a man that hung on the chimney breast. It was obvious that he was a relative of Lord Grave, as he had the family eyebrows and the same slightly grumpy demeanour. "See if you can make him move a little, Lucy."

Lucy slipped out of her armchair and stood facing the portrait. Uncle Ebenezer had a feather quill clutched in his hand. Lucy imagined him dropping it.

"Let go of the quill!" she commanded.

Nothing happened.

She tried again.

Nothing.

Lucy huffed in frustration.

Lord Grave glanced at the portrait. "Oh dear. Uncle Ebenezer was always a terrible old snob. Perhaps that's why he won't co-operate."

"What do you mean?"

"Let's just say he thought the lower classes were incapable of performing complex magic. The great unwashed, he called them. Said they were only fit for performing circus tricks." Lord Grave took another draw on his cigar. "To be honest, I agree with him. Perhaps you're not as talented as I thought. Perhaps you've simply had a couple of lucky accidents."

"Lucky accidents!" Anger surged in Lucy. The first time she'd ever met Lord Grave she'd thought him to be a thoroughly horrible man. She should have trusted that first instinct! "I might be *lower class*, but I'm just as good as you! Better, in fact. I don't sit around all day on my backside while other people do all the work."

Lucy turned back to Uncle Ebenezer. Fury-driven adrenalin coursed through her. Her surroundings seemed sharper and brighter. She stared at the painting and imagined the quill falling to the floor.

"Do as I say, you revolting old codger, and—"

Before Lucy could finish her command, uncle Ebenezer's fingers opened and he dropped the quill.

"Incredible! Incredible!" Lord Grave guffawed.

"How's that for a lower-class unwashed magician!" snapped Lucy, her hands on her hips.

Lord Grave laughed even harder, bracing his hands on his knees. Bathsheba stared at her master

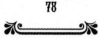

in bewilderment. "I'm terribly sorry, Lucy. I didn't mean any of it. I thought I'd make you angry to help you make the animation work. Uncle Ebenezer was a truly good man who helped many a less well-off magician develop their talents. I try to follow his example."

Lucy collapsed back into her seat and closed her eyes, waiting for her breathing and heart rate to return to normal. "Do anything like that ever again and I'm telling Bertie about you smoking!"

They both laughed again. But then Lucy had a sobering thought. "Is animation really that rare? The graverobber was able to do it too."

The laughter faded from Lord Grave's face. "That's true. You managed to take control of the angel from him, but even so, he must be a very skilled magician. We're up against someone who has the potential to be extremely dangerous."

CHAPTER NINE

THE EMERALD EYE

As soon as Lucy arrived in the kitchen next morning, Mrs Crawley thrust a cup of tea and a slice of toast at her.

"Get these down you quickly, Lucy. Lord Grave needs you in the drawing room right away!"

"What's happened?" Lucy asked between gulps of tea.

"There was a robbery last night at the jeweller's."

"A jeweller's?"

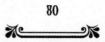

"It's not an ordinary jeweller's, of course. His Lordship hasn't gone and joined the constabulary. He'll explain. Off you go now!"

Lucy hurried out of the kitchen just as Becky was hurrying in carrying a full dustpan. The two of them collided and the contents of the dustpan tipped out on to the floor.

"You nincompoop!" Becky yelled.

"Sorry. Can't stop, Lord Grave wants me!"

Becky replied with something very rude, which earned her a sharp rebuke from Mrs Crawley.

Lucy left them to it. When she reached the drawing-room door, she paused to shake a sprinkling of the dustpan's contents off her jacket.

When she went into the drawing room, Lucy was pleased to see that Lord Grave was looking much better today. He was sitting at his desk fully dressed. He wore a new top hat to replace the one the angel had destroyed. Lucy did notice a sliver of bandage, though, poking out from underneath it.

"We're off to the seaside. To Brighton and Roland Mole," he said.

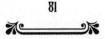

"Who?"

"He's the jeweller. Didn't Mrs Crawley tell you?"

"She said there'd been a robbery at a jeweller's. But it's not an ordinary sort of jeweller's?"

"That's right. Roland Mole deals in magical jewels and one of his most precious specimens was stolen last night."

"Do you think it's the same person who broke in here? Is that why you want to investigate?"

"No, I don't think the two crimes are linked. But we still need to look in to it. I was thinking about visiting Mole anyway so he can take a look at the notebook. Examine the jewels on the cover and tell us if there's any magic in them that we might have missed. We may as well be doing something useful while we're waiting for Reedy to arrive."

Lucy looked at him blankly.

"Angus Reedy. The bookbinder! He'll be here tonight. Are you ready to leave? Mole's relaxed all the shop's protections so that we can shortcut inside."

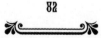

Before Lucy could reply, the drawing-room door opened.

"Father!" Bertie said.

"What is it, my boy?" Lord Grave said, suddenly looking furtive.

"You should be in bed. You're not well. I hope you're not planning on going off anywhere. You promised me you'd rest all of today. No meetings. No investigations."

"I'm absolutely fine," Lord Grave said. The tail of the bandage beneath his hat had come loose and he surreptitiously tucked it back in. "We're just taking a quick trip to Brighton, the sea air will be of benefit. Good for the constitution."

Bertie narrowed his eyes. "I know about the jewel robbery. Lady Sibyl mentioned it at breakfast."

"Well, I was going to do just a little investigating. Nothing strenuous."

"I'm coming too. Look what happened last time you and Lucy went off investigating. It'll be safer with three of us."

*

83

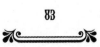

As Lucy had never been to Roland Mole's shop, and there wasn't time to fiddle about finding a suitable picture of it, Lord Grave shortcut them there. It took him several attempts to make the opening so he obviously wasn't feeling quite as chipper as he was pretending.

"I knew he wasn't a hundred per cent," Bertie muttered to Lucy. "It's a good thing I came with you."

"I can hear you, my boy. Nothing wrong with me and my hearing is as sharp as ever," Lord Grave said.

As Lucy climbed through the opening into the jeweller's she gasped at the treasures it contained. There was a vast array of glass cabinets holding jewellery made of gold, silver and brightly coloured precious stones. A dark-haired girl was busily polishing the already gleaming displays while an equally spotless small fluffy dog trotted around. Everything glittered most impressively in the light from a huge chandelier, which held hundreds of delicate, extremely thin candles. Lucy decided the chandelier must be magical; if the candles were lit by hand, the first one would have burned out by the time the last was lit.

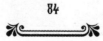

"Father!" called the girl. "They're here!"

A man stepped in through a door at the back of the shop.

"You took your time, Grave," he said in a snippy voice.

"Came as quick as I could, Mole. This is my son Bertie and my assistant Lucy."

Roland eyed them warily. "Don't like strange children in my shop. They mess around. Break things."

Lucy huffed. "We're not toddlers, you know!"

"Is there somewhere to sit, Mole?" Lord Grave asked. He was looking rather peaky.

After calling to his daughter to look after the shop, Mole picked up the fluffy dog and then led them into the back room, where he offered packing cases to sit on. Lord Grave looked very grateful for a seat, even though the cases were splintery.

"What happened, Mole?"

"It was very early this morning. Was fast asleep. A most pleasing dream about garnet necklaces. Then Precious here began barking. She wouldn't stop. So I went down into the shop. At first, nothing seemed

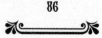

amiss. But then I realised that the Emerald Eye was missing."

Lucy and Bertie exchanged puzzled looks.

"For the benefit of you children, I shall explain. The Emerald Eye is very unique jewel. It has a particularly exquisite magical quality; it enhances sight, as the name suggests. Look at an object through the Emerald Eye and you can see the most tremendous detail. It's very valuable and one of my most requested jewels."

"Mole rents out his jewels to other magicians when they need them for magical purposes," Lord Grave explained.

"So the Emerald Eye is a microscope? They're common enough," Bertie said.

"There is no comparison," Mole replied huffily. "Use of the Emerald Eye can reputedly even give a blind person sight. Can your microscope do that, young man?"

"No, but one day science will find a way to—"

"Mole, perhaps you could show us where the Eye was kept?" Lord Grave interrupted.

"Certainly." Mole led them back out into the shop where his daughter was still cleaning. He showed them a display cabinet, which stood in the centre of the shop floor. The jewels beneath the glass were arranged in a display of ever decreasing circles, at the centre of which was a setting for single jewel. The setting was empty.

"What did the Emerald Eye look like?" Lucy asked.

"A beauty. Green as the freshest grass, with the most wonderful markings," Mole said, kissing his fingers.

"Do you have a picture of it, Mole?"

"It's in my catalogue. Annette, my lovely, could you fetch a copy?"

The dark-haired girl stopped her dusting. "Of course, Father."

When Annette had brought the catalogue over, Mole flicked though it until he found the page he was looking for. Lucy could see instantly why the Emerald Eye was so named. At its centre was a dark, glossy and perfectly round spot, just like the iris of a human

eye. The spot had diagonal and vertical lines running from it to the edges of the jewel, a little like the spokes of a wheel. But the overall effect was still that of an eye.

"Was it the only Emerald Eye in the world?" Lucy asked.

"An interesting question and a matter of some debate. It is rumoured that the Eye once had a twin, but it was stolen a very long time ago and no one has seen it since."

While Lucy and Lord Grave were talking to Mole, Bertie had been examining the display case. "There's no sign that it's been forced open," he said.

"Well, I know that. Don't you think that's the first thing I checked?"

"Father, don't snap. The boy's just trying to help," Annette said.

Mole looked very slightly chastened. "I just can't understand how it happened."

"Were there any witnesses?" Lucy asked.

"No. Although Mrs Crumb who runs the chocolate shop opposite thinks she saw someone in here. Early hours of the morning. A woman. But she can't be certain. She was taking in a delivery of cocoa beans and was still half asleep."

"Look, Father," Bertie said. "This was trapped in the hinge of the cabinet." He held his discovery up to the light. It was a very long blond hair.

"Well, that doesn't belong to me," Mole said, stroking his head, which was as bald and brown as an egg. "And it doesn't belong to my Annette ether."

"Anyone else it could belong to that you know of?" Lord Grave asked.

"There haven't been any blonde-haired women here in recent days have there, my lovely?" Mole asked his daughter, his voice soft and much less cross.

"Not that I remember."

"When was this cabinet last cleaned?" Bertie asked.

"We clean everything every day, although I haven't cleaned today. We didn't want to mess up any evidence," Annette said.

While the others were talking, Lucy spotted something that looked like a piece of silvery spider's web clinging to the bottom of the display cabinet. She crouched down and stared hard at it, excitement growing inside her. The shiny skeins and the rainbow-like droplets attached to them were the same as the magical trace she had found on the night of the break-in at Grave Hall.

CHAPTER TEN

A VERY PRECISE DEATH

"Look, Lord Grave, there's another of those traces." Lucy pointed at the trace, being careful to not touch it.

Lord Grave followed Lucy's pointing finger, but it was clear he couldn't see anything. "What does it look like?"

"The same as the one I saw at the break-in."

"Yes, I suppose they must all be a little alike—"

"No, you don't understand," Lucy interrupted. "It

looks *exactly* like the one at Grave Hall; I'm sure of it."

"I wish I could see it. Is it round about here, Lucy?" Bertie said, hunkering down next to her. He jabbed his finger in the general direction of the silvery skein.

"Careful," Lucy said. "You're really close to it. Don't—"

But it was too late. The instant Bertie unwittingly touched the trace, it exploded into a flurry of tiny sparks and vanished. Lucy groaned in frustration.

"What happened?" Lord Grave asked.

"It's gone."

"I'm so sorry!" said Bertie.

"Can we stop all this shilly-shallying and get on, Grave?" Mole said snappishly. "I've a business to run, you know!"

"Just wait a moment, Mole. This is important. If the two traces match, there could be a link between the robbery here and a break-in at Grave Hall. Lucy, Bertie, we need to have a very thorough exploration of this shop. See if we can find any other evidence."

They spent the next hour searching the shop, but

found no more clues. Lord Grave asked Roland Mole to take a look at the mysterious notebook, but the jeweller was impatiently dismissive. He said the jewels that decorated the cover were "common-or-garden diamonds, rubies and sapphires" with no magical qualities whatsoever.

✳

At just after eight o'clock that evening, Lucy and the rest of MAAM gathered in the meeting room, anxiously awaiting the arrival of Angus Reedy, the bookbinder.

Lord Grave took out his pocket watch. "Reedy said he would be here at twenty-one minutes past eight, so we have some time. I suggest I report back on our visit to Roland Mole and the theft of the Emerald Eye. We have three main clues." Lord Grave went on to explain about the sighting of a woman at the scene of the crime, the blond hair Bertie had found and the trace Lucy had seen.

"Did anyone think to try to preserve the trace somehow?" asked Beguildy.

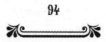

Lord Grave smoothed the end of his moustache. "I'm afraid the trace was accidentally destroyed."

Beguildy drummed his fingers on the table and smirked. "Oh, Lucy, were you a bit clumsy?"

Bertie went very red. "No. Actually it was my fault. Lucy didn't do anything wrong."

"I had enough time to look at it anyway," Lucy said, feeling sorry for Bertie, who looked rather woebegone. "I'm certain it was the same as the trace I found the night of the break-in."

"So the two crimes could be linked?" Prudence said. "But how would that explain the fact that the burglar was a man and the suspect in this case was a woman?"

Lucy had been pondering this very question herself ever since the visit to Roland Mole and had come up with an answer she thought might be plausible.

"Maybe there's a team? A man and a woman?"

"A team?" Beguildy said sharply. "That's a ridiculous idea."

"I think she could be right, B," Prudence said.

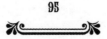

"It's an excellent theory," Lord Grave agreed.

The rest of MAAM went along with Lucy's premise too. This didn't please Beguildy one bit, judging by his expression, which suggested he had just drunk a pint of sour milk. But before he could say anything further Rivers knocked on the meeting-room door.

"Angus Reedy," he announced, ushering in a short thin man dressed in garments that were varying shades of faded black. He wore a pair of silver pince-nez on his rather large nose and carried a small leather case.

Lord Grave left his seat, went over to Reedy and shook his hand vigorously. "Thank you for coming straight here. You must be exhausted after your journey. Rivers, pour Angus a glass of wine, please."

Reedy took the glass of wine Rivers proffered and gulped it down in one before handing the empty glass back to him.

"You can go now, Rivers. I'll ring if we need anything," Lord Grave said.

"Yes, sir," said Rivers and left the room.

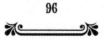

"So, Grave. Is that the object? Let me see it," Reedy said, making a beeline for the table where the notebook lay. He took a pair of white gloves from his case and donned them before picking up the notebook, which he held up to his sizable nose.

Sniff.

Sniff.

Sniiiiiiiff.

Lucy and Bertie, who were sitting next to each other at the table exchanged glances. Bertie stifled a giggle.

Sniiiiiiiiiiiiff.

Lucy let out a little snort of her own; she couldn't help it. Lord Grave gave her a stern look.

"More light!" Reedy demanded.

Lord Grave tugged the bell pull to summon Rivers back to the meeting room; he instructed him to bring more oil lamps and candles in, until the room was so brightly illuminated Lady Sibyl declared it was giving her a headache, but Reedy ignored her complaints.

"More space!" he snapped.

Lord Grave made everyone leave the table and squeeze on to the sofas grouped around the fireplace. Meanwhile, Reedy took a magnifying glass from his leather case and spent the next few minutes staring at the notebook through it. Then he closed the notebook, put his equipment back in its case and sat back in his chair.

"More wine!"

Lord Grave rang the bell for Rivers again, who brought in a fresh bottle of wine and poured Reedy a glass.

"I'll wait just outside the door, shall I sir? No doubt you'll be needing me again in a few minutes?" Rivers said to Lord Grave.

"Good idea." Lord Grave replied, sounding slightly strained.

When Reedy had finished quaffing his wine, he looked around, seemingly surprised. "Why are you all sitting there? Gather round, gather round!"

Lucy trooped back to the table with the others. They looked as disgruntled as she felt at being bossed around by this irritating man.

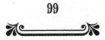

"So," said Lord Grave cautiously when everyone had settled back down at the table. "Any thoughts, Angus?"

Reedy nodded. "Foreign. Far East. Perhaps two hundred and fifty years old. Purpose: unsure. Need more time. Access to your library."

"Of course. Whatever you need." Only the twitch of Lord Grave's moustache gave any hint of impatience.

"Peace. Quiet. No people. No distractions."

"I know your requirements and it's all taken care of. I've had rooms prepared in the east wing," Lord Grave said. His moustache twitched again as he opened the meeting-room door. "Rivers, would you show Mr Reedy to his rooms?"

"Of course. Come with me, sir," Rivers said.

Reedy began following him out of the meeting room, but paused on the threshold. He turned and stared at Lucy. "That girl. Intensely magical. Astounding."

"I say," Beguildy said when Reedy had gone. "The seal of approval from a complete and utter madman. Congratulations, Lucy!"

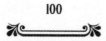

Lord Grave shook his head. "Don't be fooled. If anyone can find out the true nature of that book, Angus is the man for the job, mad or otherwise. Why don't you all stay here tonight? If I know Angus, he'll have answers for us very early tomorrow morning."

✳

Lucy woke before dawn the next day. Excited at the prospect of finding more out about the notebook, she threw on her clothes and dashed down to the kitchen before Becky had woken up. Mrs Crawley was already there, preparing a sausage, a rasher of bacon and a single egg for the guests' breakfast.

"Lucy, Mr Reedy asked that we serve him breakfast in his room at five thirty-five precisely. Would you mind taking it up to him? One cup of coffee, three-quarters full, and one and a half slices of dry toast with a thimbleful of butter. He's a very precise man. There's a clock on the wall outside his room, so you can be sure that you knock at the right time."

Lucy eagerly agreed as this might give her the chance to get ahead on news about the notebook.

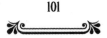

Anticipation coursed through her as she carried the tray along the east-wing corridor. When she reached Reedy's room, she watched the clock impatiently, counting down the final seconds in her head. As soon as the time was right, she knocked on the door and waited.

No answer.

She knocked again harder. Waited.

Still no answer.

Lucy checked the clock. It was now five thirty-six. Perhaps Reedy wasn't such a precise man after all. Or perhaps he was so deeply engrossed in his work that he hadn't heard her knocking? Lucy put the tray down on the floor before opening the door a little and peering through. The curtains were shut and the lamps had burned low. Reedy, who had his back to Lucy, was sitting at a desk facing the window. Although when Lucy looked closer, he was more slumped than sitting. He must have fallen asleep on the job! Lucy picked up the tray and went inside.

"Good morning, Mr Reedy! Here's your coffee and toast! All very precise, just as you like it!" Lucy

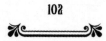

placed the tray on the desk. "Shall I open the curtains?"

But Reedy didn't reply.

A bad feeling began to grow in the pit of Lucy's stomach. She drew back one of the curtains. The window had been smashed and glass was scattered over the desk. The curtains billowed into the room, catching the three-quarters-full coffee cup and knocking it to the floor. Lucy noticed a suspiciously dark and sticky patch on the carpet.

"Mr Reedy?" Lucy tapped him on the shoulder. Then she touched his hand. Ice-cold. His arm suddenly slid off the chair making Lucy gasp. When she caught a glimpse of silver, she finally understood why Reedy wasn't moving. Someone had plunged a dagger very precisely into his heart.

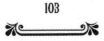

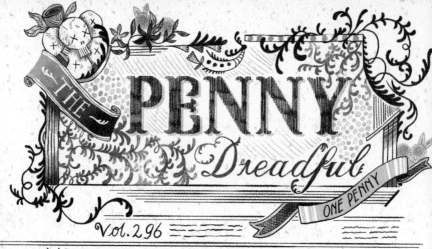

THE **PENNY** *Dreadful*

ONE PENNY

Vol. 296

MURDER AT GRAVE HALL!

ZOMBIE GIRAFFE THOUGHT TO BE RESPONSIBLE

THE *PENNY* is dismayed to reveal that there has been a murder at Grave Hall. The body, not yet identified, was found early this morning. It is not known whether the victim was a member of Lord Grave's household or a guest.

Sir Absalom Balderdash, the respected scientist, says he has long had misgivings about the exotic animals Lord Grave keeps in the grounds of Grave Hall. "We know nothing about the background of these animals. Although the zombie apocalypse has yet to reach these shores, it is possible these beasts could be harbouring the zombie virus. According to my meticulous research, giraffes are particularly susceptible and can turn very nasty once zombiefied," he said.

Our intrepid reporter Slimeous Osburn has suffered attacks from Lord Grave's animals in the past and is of the opinion that Sir Balderdash's theories have merit.

As readers will know, Lord Grave has been no stranger to controversy in recent weeks. One aspect of the case of the kidnapped children, which was solved by Lord Grave and his boot girl, Lucy Goodly, has still not been adequately explained. We speak, of course, of the matter of young Albert Grave. Albert was believed to have died five years ago at the age of seven, but was miraculously found with the kidnapped children. On page three, the *Penny* discusses whether the boy is, in fact, an imposter.

CHAPTER ELEVEN

A MOUTHFUL OF DUST

"Well, we can safely say that poor Angus is definitely dead. And of course, the notebook is gone," Lord Grave said, bending over the bookbinder's slumped form.

Lucy was sitting dazedly on the edge of Reedy's bed. She couldn't stop shivering. Bertie was perched on one side of her, awkwardly patting her shoulder. Prudence sat on Lucy's other side and was absent-mindedly holding her hand while staring wide-eyed

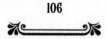

and horrified at the dead man. Lady Sibyl had gone to her own room to lie down, overcome with shock.

"Are you going to call the police?" Lucy asked.

"No. This is a magical matter and we want to keep it that way if we can." Lord Grave's face was pale and Lucy saw that his hands were trembling as much as her own. "Percy, Beguildy, can you take the poor chap out of here and put him in one of the other bedrooms?"

"I've never seen a dead person before," Bertie said as Reedy's body was carted off by the two men.

"Me neither, and I hope I never do again," Lucy replied and shuddered.

"I have," Prudence said. "My own dear parents. They died when I was only five years old."

"Prudence, my dear," Lord Grave said gently, "why don't you follow Sibyl's example and have a little lie-down?"

Prudence lifted her chin. "No. I'm not a little girl to be sent off to her room at the first sign of unpleasantness. If Lucy can bear to be here, so can I!"

When Beguildy and Percy had returned, they

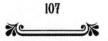

huddled together with Lord Grave to discuss the best magical method of uncovering clues. Lucy sat half listening, while what she had seen went around and around in her head. She suddenly realised Lord Grave was talking to her.

"Lucy, I'm sorry to ask, but I need you to have a good look about the room. See if you can find a trace like the two you saw before. Can you do that?"

"I think so."

"We'll do it together, Lucy," Prudence said. "You search and I'll be right here with you."

Lucy wasn't usually a holding hands sort of person, but she found it very comforting to feel Prudence's warm fingers entwined with her own as she carefully examined the room for the mysterious strands she had found the night of the break-in and at Roland Mole's. But this time there was nothing. When she'd finished searching, she rejoined Bertie and watched as Lord Grave and the others bustled about. Sparks flew as they tried various magical clue-revealing spells, but nothing seemed to be working and they kept disagreeing about what to try next.

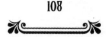

After a while, Bertie sighed and shook his head. "Look at them. Do you think they know what they're doing? What do you say to doing some proper detecting?"

Lucy was feeling a little better now so she agreed, although she felt that detecting the non-magical way would probably be a waste of time.

"So what do we do?" she asked Bertie.

"Let's divide the room. I'll take the half with the wardrobe in it and you take the half with the bed in it and we'll meet at the desk; it's roughly in the middle. We can search that together."

Lucy began rummaging around her allotted half of the room, examining everything carefully. She checked the velvet curtains that hung on the four-poster, but couldn't quite bring herself to search the bed itself. Instead she had a good look at the bedside table and the washstand and inspected the water jug.

After a while, Beguildy spotted what she was doing and took the opportunity to mock her. "What do you think you're going to find, Lucy? The murderer's calling card?"

Lucy took absolutely no notice and carried on searching.

"Oh, she's crawling under the bed now! How ludicrous, all she's going to gain is a mouthful of dust!"

It *was* dusty under the bed. Cleaning the guest bedrooms was Becky's job and she had clearly been slacking off. Lucy was about to crawl back out when she noticed a sheet of paper. It was probably just a bit of rubbish that Becky hadn't bothered to throw away, but Lucy grabbed it anyway. Just as she did so, she heard Bertie exclaim excitedly.

"Look at this!"

Lucy scrambled out from under the bed to see Bertie standing by the window holding one of the curtains. Everyone hastily gathered around him along with Lucy.

"I just need to get it free," Bertie murmured, fiddling with something caught in the curtain's tassels. He finally worked it loose and held it up. It was a gold earring in the shape of a starfish, with what looked like a diamond in the middle. Bertie handed it to Lord Grave.

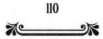

"Could it have belonged to your wife, George?" asked Lady Sibyl.

Lord Grave shook his head. "No. She didn't like earrings as a rule. Said they hurt her ears."

"One of the servants?"

"Only Becky, my housemaid, comes in this room. This can't be hers; where would she get a gold and diamond earring from?"

"It could belong to the murderer," Bertie said. "It could have caught in the curtains while she was climbing out of the window."

"So it was a woman again?" Prudence said.

"It certainly looks that way," Lord Grave said. "Which rather backs up Lucy's theory that there could be a male and a female magician working as a team."

"It's all a bit tenuous. That earring could have been there for years," Beguildy said.

Lord Grave sighed. "I think that's all we can do for now. I must go and let the relevant magical authorities know what's happened here. In the meantime, if anyone comes up with any more theories about anything that's been happening, do pipe up, as quite frankly I haven't the foggiest. Lucy, if you're up to it, meet me in the drawing room once you've had breakfast."

✳

The rest of the day passed in a rush for Lucy. She spent a lot of time closeted with Lord Grave in the drawing room, going over and over what she had seen when she'd found Reedy dead, in case there was some clue that they had missed. He finally let her escape an hour before the servants' usual suppertime, so she took herself off to the kitchen and sat at the table limp with exhaustion. Violet was off home having just finished peeling some sprouts. Lucy dearly hoped Mrs Crawley wasn't planning on making her infamous sprout surprise for supper (the surprise being the snails attached to the sprouts). Rivers was there too, reading the evening edition of the *Penny Dreadful*. It had somehow got hold of the news of Reedy's murder and was babbling on about zombie giraffes.

"I really can't bear reading any more of this rubbish," Rivers declared and closed the *Penny*. He peered across the table at Lucy.

"Mrs Crawley?" he said.

"Yes?"

"I think Miss Goodly's looking rather peaky."

Mrs Crawley put down the sprout-peeling knife she was washing and came over to have a look at Lucy.

"Hmm. You're right."

"I think she should have an early night? Maybe along with a glass of milk and a simple cheese sandwich for easy digestion?" Rivers winked at Lucy who smiled gratefully back.

"That's good advice, Rivers." Mrs Crawley soon rustled up the milk and sandwich and gave them to Lucy on a tray so she could take them upstairs with her to eat in her room in peace and quiet. But once Lucy had finished her early supper, curiosity about all the strange and horrible events needled at her, making sleep impossible. She sat up in bed and thought hard, running through everything she knew so far:

Someone was stealing grave dirt for unknown purposes.

The graverobber was an animator, but perhaps not a very good one as Lucy had defeated him or her.

There was a magical notebook (now missing) involved, but no one knew what it did exactly.

A blonde-haired woman had stolen Roland Mole's Emerald Eye, which was believed to be one of a pair.

A woman, who wore gold and diamond earrings, had murdered Angus Reedy and stolen the notebook.

Lucy had noticed what seemed to be identical web-like traces of magic at the scene of the break-in and the jewel robbery, which suggested the crimes were linked.

None of it was much to go on, and try as she might Lucy couldn't really see how everything connected. If only she could uncover more clues to help her make sense of it all. Then she remembered the piece of paper she'd found under Reedy's bed. She'd forgotten all about it! It might be important. She took it out of

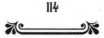

her pocket, where it had become rather crumpled, and smoothed it out. With a twist of excitement, she saw there was a drawing on it, sketched out in pencil. But then her excitement died a little. It looked like a small child's picture of a monster. It was just an outline with no features or details; the face was blank without eyes nose or mouth. At the bottom of the page, next to the monster's left foot, were two small circles and an oblong. And in the far right corner were two initials. A. R.

The excitement came flooding back. A. R! Angus Reedy must have drawn this before he died. It had to mean something! She stared closely at the drawing, but nothing jumped out at her. She turned it over and saw that two words had been hastily inked on the back. The letters were smudged, as though the paper had been unexpectedly snatched from the writer's hand. Perhaps by the murderer? But why hadn't she taken it with her? Perhaps she had dropped it without realising, and then the wind gusting through the broken window had blown it under the bed.

Lucy studied the letters more closely:

Ani − − − e − e

Lucy began to think of all the words she knew that began in *ani* and ended in *e*.

Five minutes later, she had come up with precisely nothing and she was feeling most frustrated. She turned the paper over and stared at the roughly sketched monster.

"Oh, what are you supposed to be *for*?" she said crossly.

The monster's foot twitched ever so slightly.

"What did you just do?" Lucy asked the drawing.

Nothing happened.

Lucy turned the paper over again.

Ani − − − e − e

A − n − i − m − a − t − e − m − e.

Animate me!

The paper shook in her hand as she turned it back over to the monster side. What was it that Lord Grave had said when she had tried animating the portrait of Uncle Ebenezer? *Sometimes intense emotions enable us to perform magic we didn't know we had in us.*

Well, she was certainly experiencing some intense emotion right now. She stared at the monster, trying to channel all her excitement and nervous energy into making the drawing move.

The monster began to twitch again.

"Reedy wanted you to show us something. What was it?" Lucy asked in a firm voice.

The two circles at the monster's left foot began to glow, yellow at first, deepening to green. Then they winked out before reappearing on the monster's face as eyes. Lucy gasped. Next, writing appeared on the oblong at the monster's feet. Lucy had to squint really hard to see the tiny word written there. It looked like "command". Then the oblong vanished too, reappearing on the monster's face, exactly where a mouth would be.

Lucy stared at the drawing.

The green circles, were they meant to be Emerald Eyes? Lucy remembered what Roland Mole had said about how the stolen Emerald Eye was rumoured to be one of a pair. And the oblong with the writing on, could that represent a page from the mysterious

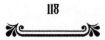

notebook? Did Angus Reedy animate this picture to show that whoever had stolen the notebook and the Emerald Eye was attempting to create a monster?

CHAPTER TWELVE

GOLEMS AND MURDER

Lucy rushed out of her room and headed off to the drawing room where she knew that Lord Grave and the others would be enjoying a pre-dinner drink. As she sped down the last flight of stairs, she saw someone lurking outside the drawing-room door. She had the sudden wild thought that it was the graverobber. Her breath caught in her throat. But her imagination was running away with her. It was just Rivers, holding a silver tray with a

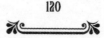

bottle balanced on it. She hurried towards him.

"Oh, Miss Goodly! Is everything all right? Why aren't you resting?"

"I need to tell Lord Grave something."

"What is it?"

Before Lucy could reply the drawing-room door was flung open by Beguildy Beguildy. "Stop loitering out there, butler, and bring that gin in. I've been waiting *hours*."

Lucy squeezed herself between the two men, nearly knocking the tray out of Rivers' hands, and skidded into the drawing room, startling everyone. Lady Sibyl dropped her glass of sherry and Bertie slopped raspberry cordial down his front while Smell choked on the milk he was lapping from a saucer.

"What is it, Lucy?" Lord Grave asked. He'd managed to hang on to his whisky and soda.

"A monster!"

"Has the child had some kind of nightmare?" Beguildy asked, calmly holding out his gin glass for Rivers to top up. It had a straw and a fussy pink paper umbrella sticking out of it.

"No. This. Look." Lucy handed the monster drawing to Lord Grave.

"Rivers, you can go now," Lord Grave said hastily.

"Are you sure you don't need anything else, your Lordship?"

"No, thank you."

When Rivers had left the room, everyone clustered around to examine the drawing. It was still animated, with the circles and oblong transforming themselves on the monster's face and then fading and reappearing next to the monster's feet before moving back to its face again in an endless loop.

"Look at its eyes; they're meant to be emeralds, I'm sure of it," Lucy said.

"The mouth," Bertie said. "It's like a piece of notepaper with something written on it. Oh, is it meant to be a page from the notebook?"

"Oh my goodness, George, they're right! It's a golem!" Lady Sibyl exclaimed.

Lucy frowned in confusion. "A what?"

"A magical monster, created out of earth or clay," Lord Grave said. "Immensely powerful and very dangerous. A golem knows nothing of good and evil; it exists simply to carry out its maker's commands. The creation of golems is strictly forbidden in the magical world and no reputable magician would even think of making one."

"I think Reedy wanted to warn us that this is what the criminals are trying to do!" Lucy said.

Beguildy peered at the drawing.

"If Angus Reedy drew that, it's a good thing he didn't attempt an artistic career," he remarked.

There was a horrified silence.

"Beguildy!" Lord Grave said. "Show some respect. A man has died here. A man who was a good friend to some of us!"

Although Beguildy failed to apologise, he at least showed a shred of decency by looking very slightly shamefaced as he took a sip of his drink.

"George," Lady Sibyl said, her eyes wide. "Mortimer Thorne!"

"I was thinking the same thing, Sibyl," Lord Grave replied.

"Mortimer Thorne? I remember that case from

when we were at school," Prudence said. "B, do you remember? That chap from O'Brien's?"

Prudence realised Lucy and Bertie were looking baffled.

"He was a very gifted animator," she explained. "He worked at O'Brien's Midnight Circus, which as you may guess is a magical circus. He had a sideshow there, animating objects. Making cups walk, tables dance, that sort of thing. Ordinary people thought it was some clever trick with clockwork or an optical illusion. The sideshow was incredibly successful. I went with some school friends once and we all thought what he was doing was terribly clever. It seems awful now, but none of us realised what a bad man he was."

"Lots of people didn't. But MAAM was never very happy with what Thorne was doing from the start," Lord Grave said. "The circus itself is bad enough, but at least they try to ensure their magic can be explained away as clever tricks. Thorne grew more and more arrogant as time went on and didn't bother to hide anything or perform magic in subtle ways."

"Is that why he went to prison, Father? For not concealing his magic?"

"No, Bertie. It's not against our laws exactly to be flagrant with magic, just against a good magician's ethics. Everyone tried to reason with him, but he wouldn't listen. He considered himself better than any of us. Wanted to be the most powerful magician in the land. It was his view that we shouldn't hide ourselves away from non-magicians, that we should show them our magic and make them afraid so they would look up to us. Even the circus folk couldn't stomach him in the end. They threw him out. So he took his revenge. One night he went back to the circus with a golem he'd been secretly making. Now that *is* against our laws. Using magic to create living things is forbidden."

"I'll never forget it," Lady Sibyl said quietly. "When we arrived at the circus to investigate, we found complete carnage. Bodies everywhere. People who had been out for an evening's entertainment but ended up never going home again. Of course, the non-magicians thought the golem was some kind of clockwork marionette controlled by Thorne, so he was arrested for murder. If Lord Grave hadn't intervened he would have been hanged instead of going to prison."

"Why did you do that, Father? You should have let him die!" Bertie said angrily.

"I don't believe in killing people for their crimes. Rotting away in prison is a worse punishment in some ways. Especially for someone like Thorne, who had such delusions of grandeur. He's been largely forgotten in the ten years he's been in prison. He must hate that."

"Is there any chance that it's Thorne behind everything that's happening? Could he have escaped?" Lucy asked.

"Very unlikely. We put many protections in place and he's guarded round the clock by magicians. We made special arrangements with the prison authorities," Lord Grave said.

Lucy frowned. "But I thought you didn't like non-magicians knowing about magic?"

"Sometimes there's no choice and we have to collaborate with the non-magical establishment."

"So what do we do next?" Lucy stared at the

animated paper golem again, watching the eyes appear and disappear from its face.

"We go to Millbank Prison. That's where Mortimer Thorne is being held. We need to question him. Perhaps he has an accomplice on the outside who knows about golem-making."

"We should visit O'Brien too, George. The circus is in Hyde Park this month; my cousin's footman went to see it. We could even go tonight."

Lord Grave took out his pocket watch. "I don't know, Sibyl. If we left now, we wouldn't arrive until around five am. That would be too early to visit the prison, too late to visit the circus."

"Couldn't we shortcut?" Lucy asked, impatient to get on the case as soon as possible.

"Shortcutting into London is tricky. Such a busy place – you might think you're shortcutting into a quiet side street and end up in the middle of a crowd," Lord Grave said. "We'd have to shortcut into countryside outside London, which can be difficult to navigate. And then of course we would still need to get from there into the city."

"Besides, I hate shortcutting," Beguildy said and shuddered. "It makes me horribly sick."

"You could always stay behind," Lucy muttered under her breath.

"Well then, I suggest we set off in a few hours and aim to get to Millbank for around nine am. We can visit O'Brien tomorrow night," Lord Grave said.

"George," Lady Sibyl said. "You're being ridiculous. You know my horses can get us there in no time! I think we need to act as soon as we can. There is a murderer on the loose after all!"

Lucy had quite forgotten about Lady Sibyl's flying horses. "That's a brilliant idea! Can we go now?"

Lord Grave harrumphed. "Well, I don't know. Might not be sensible to go haring off." His face had taken on a slightly green tinge.

"Oh, come on, Grave, admit it. You're afraid of flying, ain't you?" Smell said.

"George. I've told you before. It's nothing to be ashamed of; we all have our fears," Lady Sibyl said.

"Of course I'm not scared! What a ridiculous notion." Lord Grave's moustache bristled in

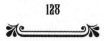

annoyance. As if to demonstrate just how scared he wasn't, he immediately rang the bell for Rivers. When he arrived, Lord Grave instructed him to ready Lady Sibyl's carriage straight away and to ask Mrs Crawley to prepare some sandwiches in place of dinner.

CHAPTER THIRTEEN

LONDON SMOG

As it was a chilly night and it would be even colder flying, Lucy ran up to her room to fetch her cloak before meeting everyone else at the carriage house. She was so eager to get on with the investigation that she was the first to arrive. Lady Sibyl's coach was parked outside and Rivers was busy harnessing the horses.

"There you are, my beauties," Rivers was saying

to them, his voice soft and caring. "Nice and comfortable, I hope?"

"Hello, Rivers," Lucy said.

Rivers turned. "Miss Goodly! Are you looking forward to tonight's flight?"

"Oh yes." Lucy went up to the horses to feed them a couple of apples she'd filched from the kitchen on her way out. "But . . . but the horses don't have wings. How are they going to fly?"

"You'll see." Rivers winked at her. "I hear you've been doing some excellent investigating? Everything's moving so fast I've quite lost track!"

"It is all very exciting, but a bit scary," Lucy said, stroking the horses' noses as they munched their apples. "We think someone's trying to make a golem!"

"A golem?" Rivers frowned. "I don't like the sound of that at all. I don't know much about them. Forbidden magic, of course. But the perpetrator must be a very dangerous magician. I do hope you'll be careful."

"Don't worry about me. I can look after myself."

"I'm sure you can. Oh, look sharp, here come the rest of my passengers."

Lord Grave, Lady Sibyl, Bertie, Beguildy and Smell joined Lucy next to the carriage. Prudence was staying at Grave Hall to keep an eye on things there along with Lord Percy, who had gone home for dinner but was now on his way back, summoned by a chit from Lord Grave.

"Are we all going to fit inside?" Bertie asked.

"That's a good point, Bertie. It is only a four-seater really and a small four-seater at that," Lady Sibyl said.

"Could we hitch the horses to Father's carriage? It's bigger."

"I'm afraid not," Lady Sibyl said. "This carriage is specially made, and all the materials are lightweight and designed for flight."

"If I might venture a suggestion?" Rivers said. "Someone could travel up top with me."

"I will!" Lucy volunteered immediately, imagining how much more thrilling it would be to sit outside the coach. The view would be incredible.

"You're a braver person than me, Lucy," Lord Grave remarked. For some strange reason he was holding a chamberpot in his hand.

✳

When everyone had settled inside the carriage, Rivers took a brush from his pocket. It began to glow like a tiny moon as Rivers ran it gently along the sides of the two horses. Sparks danced along their skin and elegant wings began to unfurl. Then Rivers carefully brushed the horses' manes and tails, which became as light and fluffy as thistledown.

Rivers stood back and studied the results of his endeavours with satisfaction. "I think we're ready now, Miss Goodly. Let me help you up into the driver's seat."

Once they were both seated and their knees covered with a thick blanket, Rivers flicked a whip lightly over the horses' rumps.

Lucy cried out, not liking to see the beautiful creatures hurt.

"It doesn't harm them," Rivers reassured her. "It's just a signal for them to—"

The horses gave a great leap into the air, pulling the carriage with them. Lucy was jolted violently in her seat.

"Take off! Grab the handrail, Miss Goodly!"

Lucy did as Rivers said, hanging on fast to the rail as the carriage bounced and jerked into the sky. But once they were fully airborne they travelled surprisingly smoothly. The horses beat their wings so fast they were almost invisible.

Lucy cautiously peered towards the ground that was now far below them. It was too dark to see much, but here and there she saw pinpricks of light as they passed over villages and farms. "Are you sure no one will see us?" Lucy asked.

Rivers glanced at her. "It's too dark. If it was daytime it would be riskier. But even then, most people wouldn't notice unless they were magicians. And of course this carriage and the horses are shielded from non-magicians, just in case."

Lucy frowned. This was something that still confused her at times. "But Bertie's not a magician, and he can see magic happening, even when it's shielded."

"Ah, well, he has magician's blood in his veins, so he's not your average non-magician. And I know Master Bertie likes to take a rational view of magic, but I think he has a trace of magical ability in him. Even if he hasn't, and even he didn't have magical blood, he might still be able to see magic. Non-magical children often can; their minds are more open than grown-ups and they can see though the shields we put up."

"So what happens if a child sees us and tells someone?"

"Oh, I think if any child starts chattering on about seeing magical occurrences, they'll be ignored, don't you?" Rivers urged the horses on faster and higher.

There was a horrible retching noise from inside the coach.

"Oh dear," Rivers said. "Poor old Lord Grave really is a martyr to travel sickness."

✳

The exhilarating flight ended all too soon for Lucy. Rivers landed the carriage in farmland just outside

London before taking the normal non-flying route into the capital.

As the carriage rattled along the cobbled streets of London, Lucy looked eagerly around. Although she loved living at Grave Hall with its many surprises, beautiful gardens and endlessly fascinating wildlife park, she hadn't realised until now how much she missed the city, which she was used to visiting regularly. Everywhere was still abuzz. Light and laughter spilled from nearby taverns and carts rumbled by carrying meat and fruit to the markets, which would open in the early hours of the morning. Being in London again also made Lucy think rather wistfully of her parents. She hoped they were behaving themselves in Venice and not getting into any awkward scrapes. Perhaps they would come home soon and she could arrange to visit them.

"Here we are, Miss Goodly. The finest magical hotel in London. Well, it would be the finest – it's the only one!" Rivers said, reining the horses in at the entrance to Wistman's Hotel, which stood on the corner of two streets. Lucy's first impression of the hotel was that everything about it was very pointy, from the shape of the windows and doors to the spiky turrets that sprouted from its roof.

Rivers clambered down from the driver's seat before helping Lucy down. Then he hurried to open the carriage door for Lady Sibyl and the others. Lord Grave still looked rather queasy.

Lady Sibyl led the small party through the doors of Wistman's and hurried up to the reception desk. She was still dressed in her evening clothes and wore her favourite peacock feathers in her piled-up hair. The concierge appeared to know Lady Sibyl as after a brief exchange, which involved lots of *Yes, my Lady. I see, my Lady* on the part of the concierge, Lady Sibyl sallied forth again, beckoning everyone to follow her up the wide, sweeping staircase. At the same time, footmen scurried out to collect the luggage from the carriage. Lucy wondered what they would make of Lord Grave's chamberpot, and hoped he had magically cleaned it and not left it for the poor footmen to deal with.

Once everyone was settled in their various rooms

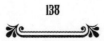

(Lucy was in one of the turrets), they met in the grand sitting room that was part of Lord Grave's suite to discuss the next steps in the investigation. Lord Grave explained that MAAM's relationship with O'Brien's Midnight Circus was frosty, due to the fact that the circus folk operated on what Lord Grave called "the fringes of ethical magic". After some thought, he decided Lucy and Bertie should handle the circus part of the investigation.

"They may be more receptive to youngsters. But I'd like Smell to go with you for safety's sake."

"I'm not going to no circus," Smell said.

"Why?" asked Lucy.

"I'm a talking cat! They'll kidnap me and use me for some kind of sideshow!"

"Don't be ridiculous! You're a member of MAAM; they wouldn't dare!" Lord Grave pointed out.

"Don't worry, Smell," Lucy said. "You can hide under my jacket. I'll make sure no one sees you."

"At least someone cares about my welfare. Any chance of a spot of supper before we go?"

✳

When Lucy (with Smell under her jacket) and Bertie were walking down the steps of Wistman's, they bumped into Rivers. He was looking rather damp.

"You timed that right," he said. "It's just stopped raining."

Lucy stifled a giggle.

"What is it, Miss Goodly?"

"Your face, you've got black smudges on your cheek!"

"Drat it!" Rivers pulled out his handkerchief and wiped his face. "That's the trouble with London. All that smog. Even the rain's dirty! Where are you two off to?"

"O'Brien's Midnight Circus. Why don't you come with us?"

"I don't really approve of that circus to be honest, Miss Goodly. But thank you for asking. Have a good night!"

"I don't like that man," Bertie said as Rivers went inside the hotel.

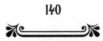

"Why? He's really nice. Very kind to everyone. And he's really good with animals."

"Smarmy is the word I'd use for him," Bertie muttered.

CHAPTER FOURTEEN

O'BRIEN'S MIDNIGHT CIRCUS

As they approached Hyde Park, Lucy could see the huge white circus marquee. It seemed to glow against the night sky and she wondered if the material contained some sort of magic. Crowds of people milled around the stalls and sideshows that were clustered nearby. There was a stand selling candyfloss and freshly made toffee, fortune-telling tents, a hall of mirrors and many other attractions that Lucy dearly wanted to stop and visit. But there was no

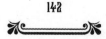

time to do so as a man at the entrance to the marquee was gesturing wildly for people to get themselves inside.

"Roll up, roll up, we're about to start!" he shouted. He was very tall and wore an eye patch over his left eye. His beard was white with grey tips and was so long he wore the end thrown over his shoulder to keep it from dragging in the dirt. A young woman in a top hat whose bright red lips matched her hair stood next to him collecting the entrance fees.

"That'll be thruppence each, duckies," she said as Lucy and Bertie approached.

Lucy handed over the money and she and Bertie went inside.

"There must be hundreds of people here," Lucy said to Bertie as they searched for some free seats. She had to raise her voice in order to be heard above the hum of excited chatter.

Just as they had managed to squeeze into a space between a noisy family and two young girls, the lights in the big top lowered until all that could be seen was the centre of the tent, which was encircled by hundreds of flickering candles.

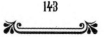

For the next two hours, a myriad of acts performed. Lucy's favourites were the knife-throwing, where the knives twirled and circled around the circus tent before hitting their target; a woman who could fold herself up to fit in a tiny jewelled box; and the trapeze artists who worked without trapezes.

"That was amazing," Lucy said, when it was over and they were leaving the big top with the rest of the audience, who were all gossiping about the marvels they had seen.

"It's very clever, I have to admit," Bertie replied.

Lucy smiled to herself. She could tell that Bertie was having difficulty coming up with what he would call a *rational explanation* for the wonders they had seen.

"Oi, you two. Get that stardust out of your eyes. You're 'ere to do a job, remember?" Smell reminded them from beneath Lucy's jacket.

"Yes, you're right. We need to find O'Brien," Bertie said.

"Look, let's ask those two where we can find him." Lucy pointed at the woman with the top hat and the man with the over-the-shoulder beard, who were standing watching the chattering, laughing people filing past. Lucy and Bertie pushed their way over to them.

"Excuse me," Lucy said.

"What is it, duckie?" the woman said.

"We wanted to find Mr O'Brien. Could you tell us where to go please?"

The bearded man frowned. "And why would you be wanting to do that?"

Lucy decided to stick as closely to the truth as she could. "We need to speak to him about someone who used to work here, Mortimer Thorne?"

The man and the woman exchanged glances. The bearded man peered more closely at Lucy. "What do you need to know?"

Bertie cleared his throat. "There's been a murder. The victim knew Mortimer Thorne. We thought maybe the murderer is someone they both knew. If we talk to Mr O'Brien, he might be able to give us information about Thorne's other associates, which might yield some clues."

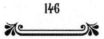

"Why are two kids investigating a murder?" the man replied. "Wait a minute. You look familiar, boy. I saw you in the *Penny Dreadful*. You're Lord Grave's son! So MAAM has sent you to nose around?"

"We've been sent to *nose around*," Lucy said sharply, "because Lord Grave thought the circus folk might be less hostile to us and we might be able to persuade you to help us try to solve the murder. Seems he was wrong. We'll just be on our way."

"Herbert. We should help if someone's been killed," the red-lipped woman said.

Herbert grunted. "Maybe. I suppose D— *Mr* O'Brien can decide whether to speak to them or not. Come with me."

He led them round the back of the big top where the members of the circus had parked their various caravans. A complicated pathway of wooden boards formed a makeshift pavement over the muddy ground. Lucy and Bertie had to carefully watch where they put their feet and so made quite slow progress. But Herbert strode along without pausing, until he reached a very brightly painted caravan. It had lacy curtains at the window and there was a reddish glow coming from the interior.

"Wait here," Herbert said. He smoothed his beard before knocking at the caravan door and going inside. A few moments later, he reappeared.

"O'Brien can give you five minutes," he said, ushering Lucy and Bertie (and the concealed Smell) up the wooden steps and into the caravan.

When Lucy stepped inside the caravan, she was surprised. She'd always imagined caravans would be cramped, spartan, a bit damp and basically not very pleasant places. But this was spacious, warm and dry. It even seemed bigger on the inside than the outside.

In the middle of the caravan was a blue velvet chaise longue. A young woman was curled up on it. She looked very elegant yet slightly eccentric, and was dressed in black satins and colourful scarves. Her black hair was most unusual; it was as straight as Lucy's own but much shorter, as short as a boy's, and cut into sharp points round each ear, giving her an elfin look.

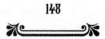

"Hello there. I'm Diamond O'Brien. I understand you're Lord Grave's son?" Diamond gave Bertie a sharp look that told Lucy there was little love lost between this woman and his Lordship.

"That's right. And this is Lucy Goodly. We were hoping to speak to Mr O'Brien?"

Lucy winced. "Bertie," she said warningly. "I think—"

Bertie bumbled on regardless. "Are you his sister?"

The woman frowned.

"Or his wife?"

The frown deepened.

"I'm sorry," Lucy said to Diamond. "He can be woefully ignorant sometimes."

Bertie glared at Lucy, looking very taken aback. "Woefully—"

"This is the owner of the circus, Bertie," Lucy continued. "Men aren't necessarily in charge of everything you know."

The woman's frown vanished and she laughed. "You tell him, darling!"

Bertie gasped and then turned the deepest red

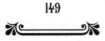

Lucy had ever seen a person blush. He hid his burning face in his hands. "I'm so sorry!"

"Don't worry. It's not the first time and I'm sure it won't be the last. To be fair, a Mr O'Brien did used to run the circus; he was my father. I took over when he died. Now, what is it you wanted to see me about? Oh, Lucy! Is that a cat under your jacket? I can see an ear poking up. Do let him out. I adore cats. Such sweet animals."

Glad to deflect some of Diamond's attention from Bertie's cringing embarrassment, Lucy unbuttoned her jacket to allow Smell to leap free. He gave himself a shake and sneezed. The violence of the sneeze caused a similar sound to emanate from his rear end.

"Oh, but he's so unusual! Unique, in fact!"

Despite Diamond's attempt at enthusiasm, Lucy thought the she looked disappointed. It was understandable. With his one eye, one and a half ears, truncated tail and tendency towards whiffing unpleasantly, Smell hardly deserved the epithet "sweet".

"What's his name?" Diamond asked.

"Smell."

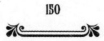

Diamond threw back her head and laughed uproariously. "What a wonderful name!"

"Not sure I agree," Smell said.

"And he talks!" Diamond clapped her hands together. "How enchanting!"

"If we could just ask you some questions?" Lucy said, wanting to get things back on track.

"Herbert said you wanted to talk about Mortimer Thorne," Diamond said, now looking more serious and rather anxious. "I'm not sure I want to talk about him. It's simply too terrible."

"Please," Lucy replied, "we just want to know about anyone who worked with him or was friendly with him."

"Very well. He didn't have many friends that I know of, to be honest. He was a difficult man, to say the least. The two he worked with most closely were Dazzling Dolly and Jerome Wormwood. They were his assistants," Diamond said. She stopped, looking rather startled. "Herbert said there's been a murder. Are they implicated?"

"We don't know yet. Are they still working here?"

"No, my darling. When Thorne built that vile *thing* and it killed all those people, Dolly and Jerome both went to jail for a while too as his accomplices. But when it became clear that they'd had no idea he had been creating a golem, they were released. As you can imagine, both of them were in an awful state. Jerome particularly. He was an orphan, you see, and I think he saw Thorne as a sort of father figure. Anyway, he went abroad, and as for Dolly, she gave up magic altogether. To be honest she was a very weak magician anyway. She was the first magician in her family and they're often poor specimens."

Lucy couldn't help be needled by Diamond's suggestion that being the first magician in a family might mean being be a lesser magician, but as she didn't want to start an argument she said nothing.

"So where's Dolly now?"

"Oh, she runs an inn. The Charm Inn."

"But I know her! Dolores Charm? She's a *magician*?" Lucy and her parents had often stayed at the Charm Inn during the period when Lucy was cheating at poker to keep the three of them fed and

housed. Mrs Charm had always seemed a normal if slightly over-talkative woman. It seemed impossible that she was a magician. But then again, Lucy would have said that about herself just a few weeks ago.

"As I said, she is a very weak magician. Without Mortimer Thorne she didn't really have a place in the magical world."

Bertie, whose face had calmed down now to a bright pink, ventured a question. "And what about Jerome Wormwood? Is he still abroad?"

"I'm not sure. We were rather close once. We're about the same age. Well, I'm a little older, I admit. He used to write to me. Then about a year ago, the letters stopped. I know he'd been ill with malaria, so he could be dead I suppose. He was such a nice boy. Handsome too. The most stunning white-blond hair I've ever seen." Diamond sighed wistfully.

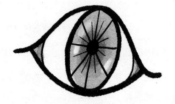

CHAPTER FIFTEEN

A DEN OF INIQUITY

"So what have we got so far? One of Mortimer Thorne's former assistants running the – what was it again, Lucy?" Lord Grave said the next morning, when MAAM had reconvened to discuss progress.

"The Charm Inn. It turns out that I know her. I've stayed there a few times."

"I've heard of it. A proper den of iniquity. Were you on your uppers, little Lucy?" Beguildy said.

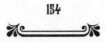

"Beguildy, stop sniping at the girl! What about this Wormwood chap?"

"Diamond O'Brien says he went abroad. He used to send her letters, but they stopped about a year ago. She says he was ill before that with malaria," Lucy explained.

"So he could be dead." Lord Grave said, steepling his fingers under his chin. "Which means our only lead at the moment is this Mrs Charm. As you know her, Lucy, I think you should call on her while Sibyl and I go to visit Thorne. Beguildy, you go with Lucy."

"Is there really any need?" Beguildy said.

Lucy folded her arms mutinously. "I'm not going with him!"

Lord Grave's face reddened dangerously. "You'll both do as I say. You need to learn to get along and work together. You're meant to be part of a team!"

There was a tense silence.

"Very well," Beguildy said.

"If I have to," Lucy snapped.

"I want you both to book rooms there and stay there for the night."

Beguildy looked as outraged at this as Lucy felt, but neither of them dared argue.

"Pretend you don't know each other, obviously. Lucy, see if you can wangle your way into Mrs Charm's living quarters. Have a look around."

Lucy nodded. "Am I allowed to tell her I'm magical? And that I know she is? Maybe I could pretend that I'm visiting her for advice. Diamond O'Brien told us Mrs Charm was the first in the family to be magical, the same as me. So we have something in common."

"Good. Good approach. That's settled then. You and Beguildy will move into the Charm Inn."

✳

Fifteen minutes later, Lucy and Beguildy were walking in not very companionable silence to the Charm Inn. Lucy suspected Beguildy was seething as much as she was. When they turned on to Masham Lane, the run-down street where the Charm Inn was situated, he stopped.

"You should book in first. I'll go in there for half an hour or so." Beguildy pointed to a coffee house

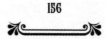

on the other side of the street. Lucy agreed readily, relieved be rid of Beguildy's company for a while.

The Charm Inn was everything Lucy remembered and less. Less clean, less fragrant and overall less welcoming. She couldn't help feeling sorry for her former self, who'd had to stay for days on end in such a grotty place. There was no one behind the tatty wooden shelf that passed as a reception desk, so she picked up the rusty handbell that stood on the shelf and rang it. There was the flip-flapping of slippers, which heralded the arrival of Mrs Charm from the back room. Perhaps it was a hangover from her circus days, but Mrs Charm was very fond of a feather boa or two. Or even three, which was the number she was wearing today, all in eye-wateringly bright shades of green, red and yellow.

"Lucy Goodly! As I live and breathe! How lovely to see you again!" Mrs Charm smiled broadly, which made Lucy feel a tiny bit queasy. Mrs Charm's own teeth had departed her gums a long time ago, and she wore a false wooden set in their place.

"It's nice to see you too."

Mrs Charm peered over Lucy's shoulder. "But where are your dear parents?"

"Oh, they're not with me. They're abroad."

"They've left you all alone?" Mrs Charm's teeth slipped slightly in horror at this display of parental neglect.

"Not exactly. It's a bit complicated. Can I book a room, though? Just for tonight?"

"Of course!" Mrs Charm opened a dog-eared ledger and studied it. "Room four is free. The one your dear parents always reserve!"

"Lovely," Lucy said, remembering the toadstools that grew enthusiastically in the corners of room four. Nevertheless, she took the key Mrs Charm handed her.

"When you're settled in, come down and we'll have a nice cup of tea and a chat."

Mrs Charm smiled again and Lucy winced.

"That would be lovely. I wanted to ask your advice about something," she replied. Having tea with Mrs Charm offered the perfect opportunity to ask a few discreet questions.

When Lucy came back downstairs, Beguildy was

at the reception shelf, booking his room. Mrs Charm wasn't behind the shelf this time. Instead there was a girl with hair almost as silvery blonde as Beguildy's own.

Lucy took great pleasure in pretending not to know who Beguildy was. When the girl had handed Beguildy his room key, Lucy made a mental note of his room number before asking where she could find Mrs Charm. The girl directed her to the hotelier's private sitting room.

"Sit down, sit down!" Mrs Charm urged when Lucy arrived. Her sitting room was as dilapidated as the rest of the Charm Inn. The dusty velvet curtains hung half off their pole and there was no carpet on the floorboards. But Mrs Charm had made an effort and put a cloth over the table, although it was horribly sticky in places. At least the teapot and cups looked as though they had been washed as recently as a week ago. Lucy sniffed. There was a distinct smell of unwashed dog. She realised that there was a grubby-looking poodle curled up next to the fire.

"So, tell me about your dear parents – where are

they?" Mrs Charm said, when she had poured them both a cup of tea.

"They're abroad. Venice."

"Still gambling?"

"Yes. They're on a winning streak."

"Oh, that surprises me. It really does. Now that you've stopped playing with that magical card."

Lucy almost dropped her cup in shock.

Mrs Charm smiled woodenly. "Oh yes, I know all about it." She brought out a paper drinking straw, stuck it in her tea and took a long suck. When she'd finished, she wiped her mouth on the tablecloth. "Too much tea can rot my teeth, dear, so I take it through a straw to keep them nice."

"I can't believe you knew," Lucy said.

"Oh, of course. I've known you and your parents for years. I remember when you were desperately poor, too poor to even pay for a room in my own humble inn. But then everything changed. You started playing poker instead of your parents. Win after win. I was very curious. I kept saying to myself *Dolores, I'm sure there's magic involved here.* So I went to see you play one night. Saw it all. And then Lord Grave turned up, sticking his nose in. Always wants to tell the rest of us how to live, that one."

"Thank you so much for not giving me away."

Mrs Charm placed her grimy hand on top of Lucy's. "We all have to make our way in the world. Ooh. It's chilly in here, let me stir up the fire."

Mrs Charm took the precaution of removing her three feather boas before she went over to the fireplace. This seemed sensible given that one stray spark would have probably set the whole lot alight, She then picked up the poker and began rattling it among the coals, much to the annoyance of the grubby poodle, who growled. As Mrs Charm leaned over the fire, something dangled out from under the bodice of her dress. It was a green jewel, hanging round her neck on a gold chain. Lucy only managed to snatch a brief glimpse of it before Mrs Charm straightened up and tucked the necklace back into place.

But in that short time, Lucy knew exactly what she'd seen. Mrs Charm was wearing the stolen Emerald Eye.

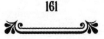

CHAPTER SIXTEEN

THE POODLE THAT BARKED IN THE NIGHT

Lucy strove to keep her expression blank as Mrs Charm made her way back to the table. Her mind raced. Could this kind but slightly feather-brained woman be a thief and a murderer who was secretly building a golem for some no-doubt dastardly purpose? It seemed a ludicrous idea, but if there was one thing Lucy had learned in recent weeks, it was that people were often not what they

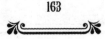

appeared to be. Her teacup rattled gently in her shaking hands. She breathed in deeply to calm herself.

"Now then, what is it you wanted to talk about?"

"Well, you see, I . . . I . . ."

Mrs Charm tilted her head. "Come along, dear, spit it out." She took another suck of her tea.

"I-I came here to talk to you about being magical. You see . . . you see . . . I'm the first one in my family to be magical and I heard that you were too."

"Goodness. Who told you that?"

Of course Diamond O'Brien had told her, but she didn't want to mention that because it might alert Mrs Charm to the fact that MAAM were investigating Mortimer Thorne. "I can't remember. But you see I'm finding it quite hard to adjust, so I thought you could give me some advice. Share experiences?"

Twenty minutes later, Mrs Charm had got completely side-tracked and was describing in detail the buffet tea served at her ninth birthday party (potted shrimp sandwiches and spotted dick).

Lucy attempted to get Mrs Charm back on track.

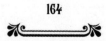

"That sounds delicious. But what about the circus? How did you end up there?"

"How did you know I used to work for the circus?"

Lucy could have kicked herself for being so careless. "Oh, I think my mum mentioned it?"

"Really? Well, I met Mr O'Brien one day when I was about twenty. I was feeling very down. You see, dear, if I'm honest, I'm not much of a magician. I tried to practise, I really did, but it always went wrong somehow. I even managed to knock all my own teeth out practising a spell. But at the same time I felt out of place in the non-magical world too. So I felt I belonged nowhere, really. Mr O'Brien, lovely man that he was, gave me a job helping with one of the sideshows."

"Fascinating!"

"I was there for ten years. But then . . ."

"Yes?"

Mrs Charm began picking at a dried-up blob of jam that was stuck to the tablecloth. "Something terrible happened. The man I was working for went too far in his magical endeavours. So I left the circus and set up my little business here. I'm very happy."

"Did you keep in touch with any of the circus folk?"

Mrs Charm stopped picking at the jam. Her hand strayed to the neck of her bodice, where the Emerald Eye nestled out of sight. "I couldn't bear to go back there. Diamond O'Brien visits me sometimes. She started running the circus after her father died, you know. That dreadful business broke his heart, all the life went out of him and he passed away soon afterwards."

"What was it that happened exactly?"

But Mrs Charm couldn't be persuaded to talk about Mortimer Thorne and his murderous golem. "Dear, you must excuse me. I have to get on now. Lots to do!"

"Maybe we could have another chat later?"

"Perhaps," said Mrs Charm vaguely.

Although Lucy hadn't managed to wheedle much information out of Mrs Charm, she was very pleased to leave the dog-scented sitting room, She hurried

off to Beguildy's room to tell him about the Emerald Eye. But he wasn't in. She went down to the reception shelf and asked the blonde girl if she knew where Beguildy he had gone.

"Oh, he said he was desperate for a cup of coffee. I think he went over the road. He invited me to go for supper with him later, but I'm on duty until midnight. He's a very good-looking gentleman. Do you happen to know if he's married?" The girl patted her white-blonde ringlets.

"Yes, he is. They're devoted to each other. Quite sickeningly so," Lucy said as she left the inn, smiling to think that she might have thwarted Beguildy's romantic pursuits. She had quite forgotten she was supposed to be pretending she didn't know him.

Out in the street, Lucy tried to act casually. For all she knew, Mrs Charm's harmless demeanour could all be an act to disguise the fact that she was a ruthless murderer. She could even suspect that Lucy suspected *her* and be watching from a window or something. So Lucy calmly crossed the road and went into the coffee shop where she found Beguildy relaxing over a cup of coffee and a large plate of fancy biscuits with green icing.

"You know they don't allow women in here, even if they dress like a boy?" he said by way of a greeting.

"Don't start! We have to go back to the hotel right now."

Beguildy rolled his eyes. "What's the hurry?"

"I've been with Mrs Charm," Lucy said in a low voice. "She's wearing the Emerald Eye!"

Much to the amusement of Lucy and the rest of the coffee shop, Beguildy dropped his cup of coffee all over his smart white breeches.

✳

Back at the Wistman's, Lord Grave held a crisis meeting.

"If only Lucy hadn't totally failed to wring information out of this Charm woman," Beguildy said, dabbing at his breeches with a damp cloth.

Lord Grave was striding around the room. "Lucy has done very well, Beguildy. Better than Lady Sibyl and I. Mortimer Thorne refused to even see us. If Lucy

had pressed too hard, our suspect could have got the wind up and decamped. We have to move carefully."

"It's a bit odd, though," Bertie said. "If I'd just stolen a valuable jewel I don't think I'd wear it. I'd hide it away somewhere. Especially if I'd murdered someone into the bargain. Lucy, you sure it *was* the Emerald Eye?"

"As certain as I can be. It was just like the catalogue sketch Roland Mole showed us."

Lord Grave frowned thoughtfully. "I'm going to ask Mole to come up from Brighton immediately. When he arrives, we question the woman and he can examine the jewel so that we can be certain it is the Emerald Eye. In the meantime, we don't want to arouse suspicions. Beguildy, Lucy, go back to the inn and stay the night as we planned. Arrive separately. Act normally."

✳

Beguildy set off for the Charm Inn first. Lucy waited for half an hour, then followed him. Just as she was leaving the hotel, she bumped into Rivers again.

"Miss Goodly, how are you?"

"Not bad."

Rivers looked surreptitiously around. "I saw Mr Beguildy earlier. He says he thinks he's cracked the case," he said in a low voice.

"*He's* cracked it!" Lucy said, outraged Beguildy was taking the credit.

"Ssh!"

"Sorry. It's just so annoying. I do all the work, spot that Mrs Charm has the Emerald Eye, and he tries to take all the glory."

Rivers patted her shoulder. "Don't worry. Lord Grave is a fair man; he'll make sure you get the credit you deserve."

"Thanks," Lucy said, calming down. "I'll see you tomorrow, I'm staying at the Charm Inn tonight."

"Rather you than me. Now I must get off. I have to clean Lady Sibyl's carriage yet again. It's getting annoying to be frank. She keeps flying off in it on her own. Comes back with the wheels covered in filth. I've even wondered. . ." Rivers stopped, looking troubled.

"Wondered what?" Lucy prompted.

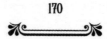

"Oh, I don't know, Miss Goodly! Perhaps she has a secret beau. I just wish they would meet somewhere less muddy! Now I'd best be off. Take care now."

Lucy made her way outside, feeling slightly perturbed. Rivers had been on the verge of telling her something, she was sure. She had the fleeting thought that perhaps he had suspicions about Lady Sibyl somehow being involved in the crimes. But it was a ridiculous notion. Lady Sibyl was devoted to MAAM and would never get involved in any sort of magical felony.

*

When Lucy reached the Charm Inn, she was not at all pleased to see Beguildy lurking in reception, attempting to woo the ringlet girl. However, he was getting short shrift.

"I would never get involved with a married man. I'm a good girl," Ringlets was saying. "I teach Bible classes on Sunday. I know Revelation off by heart."

"I swear to you, Iris, I'm not married! Who told you such a thing?"

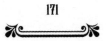

"She did." Iris pointed at Lucy.

Beguildy glared at her. "We don't even know each other," he snapped.

"I'm sorry, I was getting him mixed up with someone better-looking," Lucy said with a smile. "Could I have my room key please?"

As Lucy made her way up stairs, she heard Beguildy renewing his charm offensive. "Oh, do tell me more about your Bible study. It sounds fascinating."

*

Lucy spent an extremely uncomfortable night at the Charm Inn. As an accompaniment to the toadstools in the corners, her room boasted a damp bed and windows that rattled every time so much as a mouse scurried along the street below. At around half past four in the morning she gave up trying to sleep and decided to do some investigating instead.

She quickly dressed, lit the stub of candle that was in the crusted candlestick that belonged to the room and crept downstairs, heading for Mrs Charm's

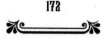

sitting room. She paused outside the door and listened carefully. When she was certain the room was empty, she went inside. Her candle guttered out, but luckily a dim light from the streetlamp outside filtered through the dirty window. Lucy had just begun leafing through a few papers that were piled up next to the fireside chair when she heard a noise in the corridor. An odd skittering.

Mrs Charm's grubby poodle nosed the sitting-room door open. It ran over to Lucy and began barking and jumping up at her as though it was on springs. It made an impressive amount of noise for such a small scruffy canine.

"Ssh!" Lucy hissed.

But the dog didn't.

Abandoning her search, Lucy vacated the sitting room as fast as she could. Her new best friend followed her, barking more and more shrilly. It was going to wake the entire household if she didn't shut it up! Lucy bent down and patted the dog's head. "There's a good boy. Be quiet now."

To her relief the dog seemed to decide it was indeed

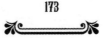

a good boy and should be quiet. It stood panting while Lucy scratched it behind the ear.

"I have to go now," she told it after a few moments.

The dog yelped indignantly.

"All right, all right." Lucy gave the poodle a few more pats and added some stroking for good measure. She soon regretted this when her hand encountered a wet, sticky patch of fur.

"Urgh!" Lucy snatched her hand away. The corridor was poorly lit by a few almost burned-out candles, which hung in lopsided holders placed haphazardly along the wall. She moved nearer to one of them, dreading to see what kind of unsavoury stickiness she'd got on her herself. It wasn't until one of the candles gave a sudden last-gasp flicker of light that Lucy realised her hand was smeared with blood.

The poodle began barking again.

THE PENNY

Dreadful

ONE PENNY

Vol. 297

A CHARMED DEATH

Mrs DOLORES CHARM, owner of the Charm Inn, London, has been found dead, believed murdered.

Details so far are sketchy, and Scotland Yard detectives are refusing to give details, but the *Penny* has discovered that Lord Grave's boot girl, Lucy

Goodly, was staying at the Charm Inn at the time of the murder. Iris Flitter, who works at the inn, told our reporter Slimeous Osburn that Goodly was found with blood on her hands. "She came out with some ridiculous story about Mushroom, Mrs Charm's poodle, being covered in blood, and that's where it came from. The police seemed to believe her. She's a very nasty piece of work, if you ask me."

Lord Grave himself was staying nearby at the mysterious members-only Wistman's Hotel. This latest murder comes barely two days after the murder at Grave Hall. We now know the victim in that case was Angus Reedy, who was found with a silver dagger through his heart. The same method is believed to have been used on Mrs Charm. The *Penny* is most concerned for the safety of citizens while Goodly and Grave remain at large.

Sir Absalom Balderdash is currently on holiday and could not be reached for comment.

CHAPTER SEVENTEEN

LUCY CRACKS THE CASE

Lucy and the others finally arrived back at Grave Hall that afternoon after dealing with the aftermath of Mrs Charm's murder. Because the crime had taken place on non-magical premises, Lord Grave had little chance of keeping things hushed up. Lucy had already been questioned by detectives from Scotland Yard who had been very suspicious of her.

"Is everyone all right?" Prudence rushed forward

as the returning travellers wearily trudged into the drawing room. She looked most anxious. "I'm so relieved you're safe and well. That awful man from the *Penny* has been to the house, banging on the door asking endless questions. Vonk tried to get rid of him, but in the end I told him to go away myself. I was rather too rude perhaps?"

"If you mean that dratted man Slimeous Osburn, you couldn't possibly have been too rude, Prue. It is a confounded nuisance that we couldn't keep this mess out of the papers," Lord Grave said.

"So what do we do now, Father?" Bertie asked.

"We redouble our efforts to identify the culprit before anyone else is killed. But first of all I want to take the precaution of fully securing Grave Hall from intruders, magical or non-magical. Will you help me, Percy? Prudence and Sibyl too. We'll divide the house up between us and meet back here in say an hour? Lucy, Bertie, while we're gone, I'd like you to put your thinking caps on. Go through everything that we know so far, everything that's happened. You might spot something that we've missed."

"I've kept meticulous notes," Bertie told Lucy when everyone had gone with Lord Grave to secure the house. "They're in my room. I'll just go and fetch them."

Lucy sank into a chair next to the fire, which had been lit because the September afternoon was chilly. Despair and fear were swishing around inside her. Despair because they seemed no nearer to solving the case. Fear because there was a murderer on the loose who had a fondness for plunging daggers into people's hearts. And even worse than that, the murderer might have a golem very soon. The thought of coming face to face with such a creature made her feel weak with dread. Lucy was a brave girl, but even she could only take so much!

✳

Because she'd had such a disturbed sleep Lucy couldn't help dozing off for a few minutes. The next thing she knew, she was being shaken awake.

"Miss Goodly?" Rivers said.

Lucy snapped awake. "What is it? Has something happened?"

"In a manner of speaking, yes." Rivers looked as awful as Lucy felt. Worse, in fact. His blue eyes had lost their normal spark, his jacket was crumpled, and even his hair had lost its usual stylish floppiness and was hanging in strings over his forehead, as though he'd combed it with one of the porcupines from the wildlife park.

"I was cleaning Lady Sibyl's carriage yet again and I found this," he continued in a voice that sounded very shaken. He showed Lucy what lay in his palm.

An earring in the shape of a starfish with a diamond at its centre.

Lucy stared at it, aghast. "It's the same as the one we found when Angus Reedy was murdered! Does this mean Lady Sibyl is the murderer? That can't be possible!"

"Oh, Miss Goodly, I wanted to tell you my suspicions when I bumped into you at the hotel. Her Ladyship has been acting very strangely the last few weeks. I'm a good servant. I keep my employer's business private. But the fact is . . . the fact is . . ."

"You must tell me, Rivers. What is it?"

"Little things, Miss Goodly. Muddy shoes when she says she hasn't been out. And, as I told you before, she's been off in the carriage without me a few times, flying alone and I don't know where to. Coming back with the carriage in a state. She went off somewhere the evening before you and Lord Grave visited Brighton."

Lucy remembered her earlier fleeting suspicion about Lady Sibyl and how she'd dismissed it. "But Lady Sibyl's so devoted to MAAM. If she is the villain, she must be a really good actor."

"I want to be wrong, believe me, Miss Goodly." Rivers looked very much as though he was going to burst into tears. Lucy very much hoped he wouldn't.

"You said you've cleaned the outside of the carriage lots of times lately. When was the last time you cleaned out the inside?"

Rivers shook his head slowly. "I'm not sure. There's been so much going on. I must confess it's been a few days. Probably not since before I gave the Beguildys a lift to their friend's house. That was the

night you and his Lordship were attacked by the stone angel."

"And have any other ladies, apart from Lady Sibyl, been in the carriage since then?"

"No. Only Prudence Beguildy."

"So then, it's possible that the earring belongs to Prudence, not Lady Sibyl?"

"You're suggesting Miss Beguildy is the culprit?" Rivers stared at her. "I-I— obviously I would be most relieved if Lady Sibyl is innocent. But even so . . ."

Lucy could hardly believe what she was thinking herself. Could Prudence really be the murderer? Prudence, who had been so kind when her brother had been so nasty? And who had comforted her on the morning of Angus Reedy's murder? Lucy peered at the starfish earring again. Now she thought about it, it *was* something Prudence might wear, given her fondness for sea-related accessories. But if Prudence was the perpetrator, what about the night in the graveyard when Lucy had battled with the graverobber over control of the stone angel? She was certain that had been a man, even though she had never seen him clearly. And the person who broke into Grave Hall and tried to steal the notebook, injuring Vonk in the process, who was clear that the attacker was male. Unless . . . unless . . .

"Prudence wasn't acting alone!" Lucy exclaimed. "It's her and Beguildy working together! Rivers, when I suggested that maybe the crimes were committed by a man and a woman working as a team, Beguildy was very quick to rubbish my idea. Maybe that's because I was on to them! And it could all add up, it really could. The two crimes at Grave Hall, they could have made it look as though someone had broken in."

"An inside job? You have a very devious mind, Miss Goodly," Rivers said admiringly. "And of course Beguildy was at the Charm Inn. So he had plenty of opportunity to do the dreadful deed on poor Mrs Charm."

"Exactly!" Lucy said. "And then the jeweller's. Roland Mole says a woman was seen in his shop the night the Emerald Eye was stolen. That could have been Prudence."

"Yes, it could!" Rivers said. He looked excited now that his mistress was seemingly in the clear. "I must say it's fiendishly clever of them to alternate the perpetrator like that. Designed to cause maximum confusion."

"They won't feel so clever soon! We have to find Lord Grave, get him on his own, tell him what you've found and what we think it means." Lucy headed for the door, but Rivers put his hand on her arm to stop her, the excitement fading from his face.

"Wait. Wait. We can't go storming in accusing members of MAAM of serious wrongdoing. There's a chance that we're dreadfully mistaken. And we don't know *why* the Beguildys are building a golem. Do you have any ideas?"

Lucy thought hard. "Maybe one of the other clues we've collected so far would explain it?"

"And what are they?"

"Let's see. The night of the break-in, there was nothing much apart from a magical trace that I found – a strange web-like thing. There was one at the jeweller's too. No one else could see them."

"Intriguing. But not much to go on. Any other clues at the jeweller's?"

"No. Wait, yes. I'd forgotten. Bertie found a blond hair trapped in the hinges of the cabinet the Emerald Eye was taken from. Oh!"

Rivers was watching her intently "What is it?"

An idea had jolted to life in Lucy's brain. She paused for a moment, letting the tendrils of her thoughts come together. "Maybe this is a mad idea. It's something Diamond O'Brien said. About Jerome Wormwood."

"Who?"

"He worked at the circus. He was Mortimer Thorne's assistant. Thorne's in prison for making a golem. Diamond said that Jerome Wormwood had white-blond hair. Just like Beguildy's. Rivers, what if Beguildy Beguildy is Jerome Wormwood and the hair Bertie found was his? Diamond said he vanished about a year ago. Smell told me that the Beguildys only joined MAAM a few months ago. What if Jerome Wormwood took on a new identity and became Beguildy Beguildy?"

Rivers stroked his chin thoughtfully. "But what about Prudence Beguildy? Did this Wormwood fellow have a twin sister?"

"Diamond said he was an orphan, but that doesn't mean he couldn't have had a twin sister, does it? They could have been separated when they were orphaned, sent to different places to live, then later come together again when they grew up. And the Beguildys are actually orphans! Prudence told me that their parents died when they were both very young!"

Rivers shook his head. "I don't know. It all seems a bit far-fetched. Even if you're right, it still doesn't explain why Beguildy would build a golem."

Lucy had already anticipated this question. "Wormwood was devoted to Thorne according to Diamond. Thorne's stuck in prison for the rest of his life. So maybe Wormwood wants to rescue him?"

"Ah. I see! Wormwood could use the golem to free Thorne? Is that what you're saying? It's quite an idea, Miss Goodly!" Rivers chuckled slightly and ran his hands through his hair.

"But it *is* possible."

"Perhaps so, but I think we should do a little more discreet investigating before we share this theory with anyone else. Then we can present a cast-iron case."

"But what sort of investigating?"

"We could shortcut to the Beguildys' residence. Vonk told me you're a dab hand at that sort of thing. We can have a quick look around. See if we can find any incriminating evidence about the whys and wherefores of it all. Something to really nail the perpetrators so they can't squirm out of it. What say you, Miss Goodly?"

"I say yes! But I don't know anything about the Beguildys' house. I need to at least know what it looks like to be able to make the shortcut."

"Don't worry. I've been there a few times with her Ladyship. I can describe it to you in lots of detail. That would work wouldn't it?"

"I can try."

"Right. Now there's an abandoned outbuilding in the grounds, we could aim for that. Less chance of being seen by the Beguildys' servants that way."

Rivers described the building to Lucy. A disused

stone cowshed, long and low with a mossy roof, set in the grounds of the Beguildys' house.

Lucy closed her eyes and imagined as hard as she could. But nothing happened. She tried again.

"Come *on*, Miss Goodly," Rivers said, sounding uncharacteristically testy when Lucy had tried and failed to make the shortcut the second time.

"I can't do it!"

"Try. Just once more. Really focus. That old cowshed still has the whiff of cow about it, if that helps."

Lucy gathered up her energy and tried again, even though she was sure she was wasting her time and they would be better off finding Lord Grave and telling him what the Beguildys had been up to. But to her surprise and excitement, after a few moments of intense concentration, the sparks that heralded the forming of a shortcut began fizzling and sparkling. Seconds later it opened. Once it got going, the whole process was much swifter than usual, as though the shortcut sensed the need for urgency.

Lucy peered though the opening, trying to make out what lay on the other side, but everything was in

darkness, with only square outlines of light visible here and there. Perhaps this was the inside of the old cowshed and the windows were shuttered up? But how on earth had she'd managed to shortcut into it when Rivers had only described the outside?

"Let's go," Rivers said.

"Are you sure this is the right place?" Lucy asked.

"Very sure. Don't be scared." Rivers took Lucy's hand. "We'll go through together."

Lucy had a moment of misgiving, then squashed the feeling down. "All right."

Seconds after the two of them had stepped through into the mysterious darkened building, the shortcut made a sucking noise and sealed itself shut, with the usual rush of energy that ruffled Lucy's hair.

"Rivers, why did it do that?" Lucy said, perplexed that the shortcut had closed all by itself. "I didn't even—"

"No, you didn't. I did. Now let's open these shutters and see what we have here." Although it was very dark, Rivers seemed to have no trouble finding his way to one of the windows.

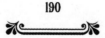

"I didn't know you could shortcut!"

"Neither did I, to be honest, Miss Goodly. Perhaps somehow you transferred your power to me in your moment of need?"

"Is that possible?"

"I don't know, but I'm very glad we made it, however it happened. These shutters! They're always so stiff." There was a creaking and scraping as Rivers wrenched the shutters open, the hinges flaking rust. Light flowed into the room and Lucy's next question died on her lips as she glimpsed the horror before her.

CHAPTER EIGHTEEN

THE REAL JEROME WORMWOOD

"The Beguildys have certainly been busy," Rivers said. "Don't worry, Miss Goodly, this thing looks harmless as yet."

Lucy inched towards the monstrous form laid out on the stone table that stood in the middle of the cowshed, preparing herself to flee at the slightest hint of movement. She could see now why the graverobber had needed to steal so much grave dirt to build the golem, which was easily twice her

height. The clay-rich earth was tightly packed and had been baked hard to a terracotta colour. Stones of various sizes were mixed into some parts of the body and the whole thing had the appearance of a very badly carved statue. The golem's head was jagged along the top, as though its maker had clumsily attempted to give it the appearance of having hair. The monster's face was completely blank with no features whatsoever. Its hands and feet were crudely formed with sausage-like fingers and stubby toes. But those sausage-like fingers were not at all comical with their fifteen-centimetre-long blades for fingernails. The feet were nothing to laugh about either; the toenails were half-moons of metal, which looked lethally sharp. Lucy was not the sort of girl who had a fit of the vapours at every opportunity, but her head began to swim at the idea of the golem becoming a living entity, and she thought she might be sick. Not wanting to look at it for a moment longer, she headed for the door and went outside.

"Come back," Rivers called.

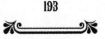

But Lucy paid no heed to him, and went out into the cool afternoon air, breathing slowly to calm herself. A fine rain began to fall. Lucy lifted her face to it, grateful for its softness and freshness. As the horrible sick feeling faded, she began to take in more of her surroundings. From where she stood, the land sloped gently upwards to the Beguildys' house. Lucy frowned. It looked wrong somehow, a strange shape, jagged and uneven. The fine rain stopped for a brief moment and a watery sun peeped out of a slice of cloud. Now she could see the house more clearly, Lucy realised why it had looked so odd. It was a ruin. Even as she watched, a flock of crows flew down and settled themselves on the exposed rafters, cawing enthusiastically to each other. Then the gap in the clouds closed and it began to rain again, this time heavily.

"Quite a mess, isn't it? I don't know how the Beguildys can bear to live in such squalor." Lucy jumped. Rivers was standing behind her. "Best get out of the rain. You'll catch your death if you stand out here much longer."

Rivers was smiling at her. But it wasn't his usual open, cheerful smile. It was less friendly, as if he was only just keeping his temper in check. Or perhaps he was feeling as unsettled as she was by the monstrous thing that lay in the building behind him. Realising she really was getting soaked, Lucy reluctantly followed Rivers back inside. There was a pile of old sacking in one corner of the cowshed. Rivers picked up a couple of pieces for them to dry themselves off with.

"It's a bit rough, but it'll do the job. What I wouldn't give for one of Mrs Crawley's freshly laundered towels right now!" Rivers said, sounding more like his usual self. When he'd finished drying his face and hair with the sacking, he dropped it on to the stone floor. Lucy wiped her own face and was about to do likewise when she noticed the sacking Rivers had discarded was smudged with black. A memory sprang into her mind. Another rainstorm, the one in London just before she went off to O'Brien's Midnight Circus with Bertie and Smell. The dirty rainwater running down Rivers' face. He'd blamed it on the London smog. But there was no smog out here in the middle of nowhere.

A terrible suspicion began to grow in Lucy. However, she made sure to nonchalantly throw her piece of sacking on top of the one Rivers had flung away. She didn't want him to know she'd noticed anything odd. Luckily, he was too engrossed in closely examining the golem.

Lucy had the overwhelming feeling that she needed to get back to Grave Hall, and fast. "We need to fetch Lord Grave urgently! Otherwise the Beguildys might guess we're on to them and make a run for it."

"Not just yet. Come and look."

This was, of course, the last thing she wanted to do, but she did as he asked and moved closer to the golem, pretending to study it carefully.

"It's impressive, don't you think?" Rivers asked.

"Yes," Lucy said. "But I still think we should leave now."

"Not yet, I said," Rivers replied, bending to examine the golem further.

Lucy's unease grew. But she didn't have to stay

here a moment longer than she wanted to. She might not have been able to shortcut to this dreadful place on her own as it was too unfamiliar to her, but she *could* shortcut back to Grave Hall. She tried not to let fear swamp her as she focused her mind on creating a shortcut to the meeting room where hopefully the rest of MAAM would be gathered by now. But something strange kept happening; it was as though she was bumping into some sort of invisible barrier. She couldn't get past it, however strongly she channelled her imagination.

"Stop that," Rivers said without looking up. The menace in his voice made Lucy's stomach flip over with fear.

"I wasn't doing anything."

Rivers turned to face her. "You remember the jeweller's? Old Roland Mole thought he had perfect anti-shortcutting charms in place, the fool. They were useless against my shortcutting skills. I've spent years honing them. I can shortcut to places you can only dream of. And my anti-shortcut charms are impregnable, unlike Mole's."

Lucy lunged for the door again, but Rivers was too quick for her. He grabbed her and pulled her away.

"I don't want to hurt you, Miss Goodly, but I need you to stay here for a while."

Rivers' hair was drying now, and the dye that covered it had turned patchy. Here and there, Lucy could see his real hair colour beginning to shine, though. It was a white-ish blond. Lucy remembered again what Diamond O'Brien had said about Jerome Wormwood. *The most stunning white-blond hair I've ever seen.*

"It was you. You're Jerome Wormwood, aren't you? It was you all along! Not Beguildy Beguildy! And Prudence was helping you!"

"I'm surprised you didn't twig before, as they say," Rivers said. "Although Prudence Beguildy had nothing to do with it. But I admit I had a little involuntary help from her and Lady Sibyl, though."

Rivers went over to a cupboard that stood in the right-hand corner of the cowshed behind the golem's head. He opened it and brought out a pile of women's clothing, including a blonde wig.

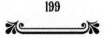

"I stole these from Prudence and her Ladyship. The stupid women have so many clothes they didn't notice me borrowing a frock here and a cloak there. Prudence wears wigs sometimes, so I took one of those too."

"You were dressed as a woman when you stole the Emerald Eye and murdered Angus Reedy!"

"I thought it would put MAAM on the wrong track if anyone spotted me. It worked more successfully than I could have hoped."

"You weren't that clever. You left the earring behind when you murdered Angus Reedy."

"That was deliberate, you silly girl. To keep MAAM thinking there was a woman involved."

Lucy remembered the sparkling web-like strands she'd seen the night of the break-in and at Roland Mole's. "What about the magical traces? You didn't mean to leave them behind, did you?"

"That was rather inconvenient, I must admit. But I wasn't to know you'd be able to see them."

In a flash of inspiration, Lucy suddenly understood the reason she'd found a trace of magic at the scene

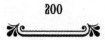

of the break-in. It must have been blown in from outside when she'd opened the front door that gusty night. "You shortcut from your room to the outside of Grave Hall and then broke in, didn't you? To make it seem like a real burglary and not an inside job!"

Rivers smiled. "Well deduced, Miss Goodly. I was a lot more careful to tidy up my magic behind me after my shortcut left a trace at Roland Mole's too."

"But why? Why are you doing all this?"

Rivers dropped the disguises carelessly to the floor. "You already worked that out, clever Miss Goodly! For Mortimer Thorne, of course. He was . . . he is like a father to me. When he was so unfairly imprisoned, I swore I would set him free. But I was too young; my skills were too immature to do anything. So I spent years improving myself. I travelled all over the world, learned many types of magic. The golem is the result of all that learning and hard work. This little, or should I say enormous, beauty is going to free Mortimer. And then we might even make a visit to Grave and the rest of MAAM. Settle a few scores. It's their fault Mortimer was imprisoned in the first place."

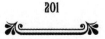

"You're really going to bring that . . . thing to life?

"No, of course not."

Lucy wilted with relief. Perhaps Rivers wasn't a reckless lunatic after all.

"You are."

"Me? What do you need me for?" Lucy said. Horrific thoughts flew though her mind. Was Rivers going to kill her? Maybe the golem needed blood to come to life!

"You see, there are some skills that even I struggle with. One of them is animation. But you . . . such talent, Miss Goodly. Grave was right to take you under his wing. You're quite extraordinary. I only wish I'd discovered you first."

Lucy stepped backwards. "No. Never! I'll never help you bring that thing to life!"

"I'd much prefer you agreed to do so. I'm not a bad man. I'm simply keeping a promise to someone I care about, the promise I made to Mortimer."

"Promises shouldn't involve murdering people!"

"I never really planned to kill anyone. But Reedy and Dolores wouldn't give me what I needed voluntarily. So I did what I had to. The end justifies the means."

"Well, I'm not going to help you reach any ends. I won't!" Despite her brave demeanour, Lucy quailed inside. Would Rivers hurt her, force her into helping him?

"Let's settle this. I want to show you something. You see I guessed you might need persuading, so I made some preparations." Rivers dropped to his haunches and grabbed a metal ring. Lucy realised it was the handle of a trapdoor. Rivers opened it and gestured for Lucy to come over.

"I'm not going near that. You'll push me down there or something."

"Why would I risk breaking your neck when I need you?"

Lucy edged closer to the trapdoor, making certain she had Rivers in plain sight all the time. A flight of narrow steep stairs ran beneath the trapdoor and into a cellar. Lucy peered through the gloom. There were two bulky shapes lying on the cellar floor. Lucy gasped as she realised the shapes were human beings.

As her eyes adjusted to the dimness below she cried out in terror and anguish. The two lifeless bodies were the people she cared most about in the world.

One was her mother, the other her father.

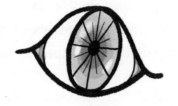

CHAPTER NINETEEN

DO CHOICE

T he cowshed tilted sickeningly around Lucy and she sank to her knees, hands covering her face, hot tears trickling between her fingers. She would have screamed, but the scream stuck in her throat. She felt Rivers patting her on the shoulder, as though he was comforting a distraught friend. The feel of his touch made her sick. She wanted to break every bone in that filthy, murderous hand.

"No, no. Don't be too upset. They're not dead,

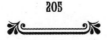

just sleeping. A simple sleeping charm. Watch."

Lucy took her hands from her face and scrubbed at her cheeks. Rivers flicked his fingers. Sparks trickled from his fingertips in a steady stream, filtering down into the cellar where they encircled her parents, who both awoke. They sat up, blinking bleary-eyed at Rivers and Lucy.

"Lucy? Is that you, my dear girl? What's going on? Why are you in Venice? This isn't the casino, is it?" asked her father.

Lucy's heart turned over at the sound of her father's voice. But before she could reply, Rivers flicked his fingers again. The sparks sputtered out and Mr and Mrs Goodly fell asleep once more. Rivers closed the trapdoor.

"So, Miss Goodly," he said as he stood up, "are you going to help me?"

And of course, Lucy had no choice but to agree.

✳

The sun had clouded over again now and the cowshed grew dark and gloomy. Rivers lit the lanterns hanging from the beams crisscrossing the ceiling. He then took out two bags from the cupboard where he had kept his disguise. One bag held the two Emerald Eyes, the other the notebook. Lucy shuddered as she watched Rivers carefully embed the jewels into the golem's blank face, positioning them where eyes would reasonably be expected to sit if the creature had been human. Lucy remembered what Roland Mole had said about Emerald Eyes being able to bestow the gift of sight. She understood now why Rivers had wanted them – to allow his monster to see. Next, Rivers took a dagger from his jacket. It was the same design as the daggers that had killed Angus Reedy and Mrs Charm; Rivers clearly had quite the collection. Lucy jolted with fear, but Rivers simply cut a slot for the monster's mouth, before stepping back to admire his grotesque handiwork.

"And now, we animate it. Or rather *you* do."

Lucy was no coward, but this was so terrifying, she couldn't help sobbing with fear. "No. Please."

Rivers sighed. "It would be easy enough, Miss Goodly, for me to deepen the sleeping charm on your parents. They wouldn't die, but they'd never wake up. And they'd have the most awful nightmares while they sleep. Endless, endless nightmares. Imagine how they would suffer. Worse than dying in many ways, don't you think? But if you help me, they'll be free to go and so will you."

Lucy gathered all her courage. She would have to go along with Rivers' demands. There was no other option.

"A few adjustments and then we're ready for the off," Rivers said, as though the three of them were about to embark on a pleasurable jaunt to the seaside. "There! Finished! Over to you, Miss Goodly."

Lucy began to focus all her energy on the golem. She imagined it sitting up, imagined the green eyes glowing with life, as they had in the sketch that Reedy had made before Rivers murdered him. She imagined harder than she had ever imagined before.

The golem's head jerked from side to side.

"It's working," whispered Rivers. "You are a most singular magician, Lucy."

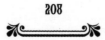

Lucy didn't bother acknowledging the compliment. She was too busy being extremely frightened, but she mastered her terror and held on to what courage she had, which felt like very little. She concentrated even harder.

The golem sat up.

"And now the command," Rivers said. He took out the notebook and wrote something in it, then tore out the page and handed it to Lucy. It said:

Obey Jerome Wormwood

"You need to put it in the golem's mouth. It has to be you as you are the animator," Rivers said.

Lucy gasped in horror.

"Oh, don't worry, it's toothless. It's a shame. I attempted several techniques, but none of them worked. Perhaps I should have tried Dolores' ridiculous wooden teeth." Rivers sniggered.

Lucy wished she was bigger and stronger, because she would have dearly loved to slap Rivers for making such a horrible, cruel joke. Mrs Charm had been a kind, harmless person who hadn't deserved to die in the horrible way she had done.

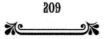

"Come along, Miss Goodly. Remember your parents."

Lucy stepped closer to the golem. She noticed another delightful detail; it was earless, although it had two holes either side of its head. It seemed to be able to hear through these holes as it turned to face Lucy when she approached. The golem gave a low-pitched snarl.

It took every scrap of courage Lucy had to slip the command Rivers had written on the notebook page into the golem's mouth. Just as she was about to do so, she noticed that Rivers had accidentally torn two pages out of the notebook instead of only the one he had written the command on. For a moment, Lucy considered putting the blank page in the golem's mouth. But it was too risky. If she tried to trick Rivers and failed, there was no knowing what he might do to her parents. So she quietly pocketed the blank page before inserting the command into the golem's mouth. The golem might not have any teeth, but Lucy still feared for her fingers, snatching her hand away as soon as the awful deed was done. In the same moment, the parchment burst into flame, burning to ash in a few seconds.

The golem made a howling noise.

Rivers stepped towards the golem's slab. "Silence, golem! I am Jerome Wormwood and you have agreed to obey me. Do you understand?"

The golem nodded slowly.

"Good. Now on your feet."

The monster swung its enormous legs over the side of the slab and did as Rivers ordered. It immediately banged its head on the cowshed ceiling, which was far too low for it to stand up straight. The golem growled in pain or anger or both and Lucy saw fear flit across Rivers' face. *He's worried he can't really control it*, Lucy thought. Was this a good thing or a bad thing?

Rivers began to make a new shortcut. In other circumstances, Lucy might have admired his skill, as he had the shortcut opened in seconds. What lay on the other side of the shortcut was a sad and terrible sight. A prison yard full of male prisoners exercising under the grey afternoon sky, overseen by four guards

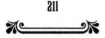

dressed in black uniforms and hats. The men shuffled dejectedly around in a circle, each wearing a hood with slits for eyes. No one seemed to have spotted the shortcut opening; Rivers must have shielded it.

"Golem, go through the opening," Rivers commanded.

Grunting, the golem did as it was told, bending itself almost in two so it could fit through. As soon as it had done so, one of the prison guards began shouting.

"They can see it!" cried Lucy.

"Of course they can! Did you think I was going to shield it? What would be the point of doing that?" Rivers said, grabbing Lucy by the arm and yanking her into the prison yard.

Although the golem wasn't doing anything in particular, apart from standing at the edge of the exercise yard growling to itself, the prison guards were yelling and shouting and blowing their whistles. Two of them roughly herded the startled prisoners against the bare brick walls of the prison, while the other two seemed to be considering approaching the golem.

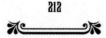

"Golem, get rid of the guards!" ordered Rivers.

The golem looked at Rivers and grunted. The grunt almost sounded like a question.

"The ones with the hats!" Rivers said, pointing to his own head and then sketching a hat in the air.

The golem grunted again and clumped towards the nearest two guards. One of them hightailed it immediately, but the other stood his ground, although that ground was soon cruelly snatched from under him when the golem grabbed him by the arm and lifted him into mid-air.

"Where is Mortimer Thorne?" Rivers shouted to the struggling, squirming guard.

"Get this thing off me! It's going to pull my arm off!" the guard screamed.

"Golem, put the nice man down now," Rivers said.

As the golem obeyed and dropped the man, the two guards who had moved the prisoners away began to approach. Rivers held up a warning hand. "Stay where you are or I'll set it on you."

The guards froze. "What is it you want?"

"I told you. Mortimer Thorne."

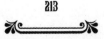

"He's kept in another part of the prison. We don't guard him."

"Tell me how to get there!"

As the terrified men blurted out directions, another guard, dressed in a bright-red uniform and brandishing a musket, belted at full speed into the yard.

"It's a golem! Get away from it!" The guard pointed his gun at the monster and fired, but the bullets ricocheted uselessly off it, as though it was protected by an invisible shield. The guard dropped the gun and flung his hand out, letting loose a flurry of sparks. But whatever spell he was trying to cast failed, the sparks dying as soon as they hit the golem's baked-earth body. The golem turned its monstrous attentions to the red-uniformed guard, who shot another shower of sparks at its chest, but again the magic had no effect on the golem. It raised its mighty arm, the talons at the ends of its fingers glinting in the sun that was beginning to break through the clouds. It snarled as it prepared to slash the guard to pieces.

"Don't hurt him. Bring him to me!" Rivers ordered.

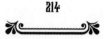

The golem picked the guard up by the leg and carried him over to Rivers before depositing him in an untidy heap on the ground.

"On your feet, man!" Rivers gave the man a not-so-gentle kick of encouragement. "Take me to Mortimer Thorne."

CHAPTER TWENTY

MEETING MORTIMER THORNE

The guard led them to a compact building, which lay some way from the main prison. It was two storeys high and had windows either side of the arched door, square on the ground floor, but round on the first. The round windows gave the building the appearance of a face with an open mouth, ready to devour anything that came near it.

"He's in there?" Rivers said.

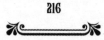

The guard nodded and pointed to one of the barred windows on the ground floor. A pale face was peering through the bars.

"Mortimer!" Rivers shouted. "It's me, Jerome! I'm coming to get you! Stand back from the window!"

The pale face vanished. Rivers turned to the golem. "Break open that window!"

The golem growled irritably. There was a tense pause during which Lucy began to fear that Rivers was about to lose control of the golem and that it would kill them all. But to her relief, the golem decided to do as it was told. It clumped over to the building and casually ripped the bars from Mortimer Thorne's window before smashing its fist through the glass. Rivers then rushed forward to help the prisoner climb from his cell to freedom.

"Mortimer," Rivers said, his voice cracking slightly.

Mortimer Thorne stared at Rivers. He had the sickly pale face of someone who had been inside for a very long time, although his dark eyes were intense and bright. He was short, but his broad shoulders and bulky arms gave him a look of immense power. He had his fists up, ready to fight.

"Jerome? It really is you?" Thorne lowered his fists.

"Yes. It's me, I'm so very glad to see you again." Rivers briefly put his arms round Thorne, who didn't return the embrace, but stood staring over Rivers' shoulder at the golem, which was now amusing itself by scraping its talons along the stone wall and watching the sparks fly.

"*You* built a golem?" he said.

"Yes," Rivers said, releasing Thorne. "Now we must get out of here!"

"Who is this child?" Thorne said, looking at Lucy as though he'd only just noticed her.

Rivers shrugged. "She's nothing. A hostage."

Lucy was about to protest, to say that she wasn't nothing! He'd needed her to bring the golem to life! But she quickly decided not to. Her common sense told her it was better that Thorne knew as little as possible about her abilities.

"Let's go!" Rivers urged again.

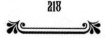

Thorne held up his hand. "Wait. I want to have a look at your masterpiece first."

Rivers smiled proudly as Thorne walked over to the golem, which looked down at him and snarled. Thorne took no notice, but grabbed the golem's thick wrist. Sparks erupted from Thorne's fingertips, scuttling like a swarm of ants up the golem's arm and on to its jagged skull, where they settled like a bright, sizzling cap.

"What are you doing?" Rivers cried.

Lucy's stomach lurched. Even if Rivers didn't understand, she did. Mortimer Thorne, a man who had once used a golem to brutally murder innocent people for no good reason, was taking control of the monster.

A second later, Rivers realised what was happening too. He ran over to his creation. "You obey me! No one else. Mortimer, you can't control it. I have this. You don't have this." Rivers took the notebook from his jacket pocket and waved in triumphantly.

Thorne made a scoffing noise. "I don't need that *nonsense*!"

"Golem!" Rivers ordered. "Come with me!"

The golem looked down at Rivers, considering the situation. It drew back its great foot and kicked him in the shin. There was a horrible crunching noise. Rivers screamed once and then fainted. Thorne threw back his head and laughed in a way that chilled Lucy. While he and the golem were momentarily distracted, she took the chance to try to dart away, but she was too slow and Thorne spotted her immediately.

"Fetch her," he commanded the golem.

A moment later, Lucy was jerked backwards, her jacket collar tearing as the monster's talons grasped at her. It dragged her over to Thorne, who studied Lucy for a few seconds. "What did Rivers want with you? You're a magician, I know that much."

"He told you. He took me hostage."

"The truth. Or the golem will cut you to ribbons!"

"He needed me to make the shortcut from Grave Hall. He's no good at them," Lucy said, too panicked to make up a more elaborate lie. But as soon as she had uttered the words, she knew she'd made a terrible mistake.

Thorne smiled. "A shortcut to Grave Hall? What an excellent suggestion. I want you to shortcut me there now. I want to see Grave. We have a lot to discuss."

"No."

"Yes!"

The golem looked down at Lucy and growled as if in agreement with Thorne, its eyes flashing erratically.

Eyes.

Suddenly Lucy knew what to do. It was a risky idea, but she had no alternative but to try it. If she gave in to Thorne's demands her friends at Grave Hall would be in deadly danger. They could all be killed.

She put her hands over her face and pretended to sob. "Oh, please don't make me."

"You'll do it. And do it now."

She might have faked crying, but she didn't need to fake the way her hands trembled as she began making the shortcut. Her heart pounded and for a

few agonising seconds, fear overwhelmed her. She clenched her fists determinedly, squeezed her eyes shut and focused on the place where she so badly needed to be. Sparks crackled around her and the shortcut began to form. At the same time, a bell started to clang from the main prison. *It's an alarm; maybe the guards are calling for reinforcements!* Lucy thought, hope surging through her. Thorne seemed to be of the same opinion and was eager to be off.

"Golem, follow behind us, let no one else through!" he said, climbing through the shortcut, dragging Lucy with him. They had barely reached the other side when a stream of guards came pounding towards them. But they arrived just a fraction too late; the golem was already hurrying through the shortcut. Once it had reached its destination, Thorne took the precaution of positioning Lucy so that it would be impossible for the guards to fire bullets through the shortcut without endangering her.

"Close it!" he yelled at her

Lucy obeyed. It was only when the shortcut was

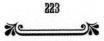

making the usual sucking noise as it shut that Thorne paid proper attention to his surroundings and realised that he was standing not in the grounds of Grave Hall, but in St Olaf's graveyard.

CHAPTER TWENTY-ONE

STONE AND EARTH

"What have you done? Where are we?" Thorne demanded, his face contorting with rage.

"I don't know! I was so scared, I made a mistake. I'm sorry!"

"Get me to Grave Hall. Now!"

"I don't think I can!" Lucy pretended to sob again and slumped to the ground as if in despair.

"If you don't make that shortcut now, I'll get the

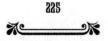

golem to . . ." Thorne looked around for the monster. "What's it doing? Golem, get over here to me!"

The golem ignored Thorne. It was standing in the last of the afternoon sun, staring at St Olaf's Church, its head tilted to one side. Lucy realised with horror that the golem was listening to the singing and organ music coming from the church. She hadn't considered the possibility that there might be a service going on and cursed herself for being so stupid. She'd now put all the people inside in horrible danger!

As Thorne fruitlessly berated the golem, the singers inside the church finished their hymn and the organ wheezed to a stop. Meanwhile, Lucy was on her feet and about to make a run for it. But then the golem suddenly turned its green eyes on her and growled. Thorne followed its gaze.

"Golem. Get the girl!" he shouted.

No longer distracted by music, the golem seemed to be more willing to heed its new master and began lumbering towards Lucy, it growls deepening.

Lucy made a swift calculation and then pelted towards the golem. This wasn't what it had been expecting and so it was momentarily confused. By the time it had gathered its miniscule wits, Lucy had whipped past it, ducked out of the way of Thorne, who tried to grab her, then doubled back and headed towards her old friend, the eyeless angel. She swiftly clambered up on to the angel's plinth.

"Remember me? You have to help me again!" Lucy concentrated desperately hard to channel her fear into producing the magic she needed to animate the angel.

The golem and Thorne were almost within grabbing distance of her now. Lucy made a final frantic effort. This time it worked. The eyeless stone face came alive and peered down at her. In a flash of desperate inspiration, Lucy took her imaginings a step further. She pictured herself *inside* the angel's body, looking through its eyeholes, controlling its limbs. There was a high-pitched ringing in her ears and everything burned bright and white as though there had been an explosion. And then Lucy was staring down on herself standing on the plinth, an empty look in her eyes. She gently picked herself up and put herself on the grass before urging her new stone body to step down from the plinth to face her two pursuers. For a few seconds, Thorne was completely wrong-footed and looked afraid. But he soon recovered. "Golem. Attack!"

The golem's eyes flashed and Lucy was sure she heard it chuckle. She'd give it something to laugh about! She flexed her stone muscles, drew her right arm back and punched the golem full in the face, exactly where its nose would have been if it had had one. Baked earth crumbled from where Lucy's stone fist had connected. For a brief moment Lucy felt sorry for the golem; she didn't enjoy hurting anyone. But that sympathy soon evaporated when the golem roared, swiping at her with its lethal claws. The talons left deep scratches on the stone angel's arm and Lucy felt burning pain as though it was her own flesh and blood that bore the brunt of the golem's assault. She was about to counter-attack with a punch on the side of the golem's head when the church bells began to peal. The golem turned and began to head towards the sound, much to the fury of Thorne, who followed it, screaming commands, all of which the golem ignored.

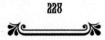

The golem and Thorne stopped by the church doors. Lucy stumped after them as quickly as her stone legs could carry her.

"If you don't shortcut me to Grave Hall I'll set the golem on the people in this church. It's your choice whether they live or die," Thorne said to her when she reached them.

Remembering how the angel had nearly killed Lord Grave, Lucy found a simple solution to her dilemma. She brought her stone fist down on Thorne's head. She was careful not to hit him too hard as she didn't want to kill him, just daze him. She judged her blow accurately and Thorne slid to the ground. The golem seemed supremely unbothered by this attack on its new master. In fact, Lucy was sure she heard it chuckle again.

She needed to put Thorne out of harm's way so she could get on with shortcutting to Grave Hall and raising the alarm. And she needed to protect the congregation inside St Olaf's. She soon spotted something nearby. The grave next to Mr Shannon's, which was protected by a mortsafe. Perfect. A

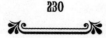

mortsafe would trap Thorne physically and also possibly prevent him casting any harmful spells if he happened to come round too soon. Lucy picked up Mortimer Thorne's limp form in her stone arms and carried him over to the grave. She laid him on the ground beside the grave and then ripped the mortsafe from the ground and deposited it over Thorne.

Just as she'd finished doing this, the church bells stopped pealing. The golem whined in protest. When the bells didn't start up again, it began bashing at the church door and hacking the wood with its finger blades. Lucy knew the door wouldn't last long. She pounded towards the church and cracked the golem hard over the head with her fist. The golem jerked and roared but wasn't deterred. It gave the door one final immense blow. The door caved in and the golem lumbered through it.

Lucy was so horrified at the danger so many people were now in that she lost her concentration. Everything wavered around her and the next second she found herself sitting on the grass next to the angel's empty plinth. Roars and screams came from inside the

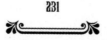

church. Lucy raced across the graveyard to where the stone angel now stood lifelessly just outside the church door. Closing her eyes and concentrating hard, Lucy tried to imagine herself back inside the angel.

Nothing.

Panting with fear, Lucy tried to animate the angel instead, but she couldn't do it; she simply couldn't do it! Crashes and more cries of panic came from the church. Lucy clambered through what was left of the door and raced inside. The congregation were huddled together behind the altar, the vicar standing protectively in front of his flock, holding up a crucifix as though it was a shield. The golem was ripping up pews and hurling them around as it made its way down the aisle, like some kind of monstrous and very bad-tempered bride approaching her groom. At first Lucy thought it was heading towards the congregation with murderous intentions. But then she realised that it was looking under the pews as it tore them up, as though it was searching for something it had mislaid. In a flash of comprehension, she understood. The

golem was looking for the music it had so enjoyed. Lucy flew up the aisle, dodging between the golem's legs.

"Sing!" she yelled at the people cowering behind the altar. "It doesn't want to hurt you; it wants more music. Sing!"

The vicar looked completely nonplussed. Lucy could understand his confusion; it wasn't every day his church was invaded by a marauding monster and a young girl barking orders at him.

"It likes music! Sing!"

"What should we sing?"

"Anything. 'Baa, Baa, Black Sheep', whatever! Just sing!"

"'All Things Bright and Beautiful', everyone!" the vicar yelled.

It probably wasn't the congregation's finest performance. In fact, Lucy was sure they were all out of tune and the organist was very shaky too. But the golem ceased in its efforts to destroy the pew it had just upended. It cocked its head, green eyes glowing with appreciation. As it soaked up the music Lucy frantically tried to decide what to do next. Then she remembered the blank page from the notebook, which she'd purloined back in the cowshed. She felt in her pocket. It was still there!

"Quick, I need a pencil!" she told the vicar.

"We need a pencil!" the vicar said to the person next to him. Word went around the congregation, who continued singing while searching their coats and bags. Thankfully, one of them soon produced a stub of pencil. Lucy then wrote *You are very sleepy. It's time for bed* on the notebook page. She ran to where the golem stood transfixed, climbed on to the upended pew next to it and slotted the page into the golem's mouth. As before, the paper burst briefly into flames. Then the golem yawned and stretched its mighty arms over its head, which began to droop. It settled itself down on a pile of wood that used to be several pews, then it curled up into a ball, put one of its talons in its mouth and soon began to snore.

As the congregation finished 'All Things Bright and Beautiful', Lucy found she wasn't feeling too bright, let alone beautiful, herself. Her knees sagged

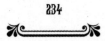

and she ended up sprawled on the cold church floor, her head spinning. She was dimly aware of a commotion around her.

"She's here, Lord Grave! She's safe!" Beguildy Beguildy shouted. "Oh no. I'm feeling sick again. I so hate shortcutting . . ."

GOODLY AND GRAVE TRIUMPH!

THE *PENNY'S* very favourite crime-busting duo has pulled off an amazing feat of detection. The talented two have solved the mysterious case of the grave robberies as well as the appalling murders of Angus Reedy and Dolores Charm, both found with daggers in their hearts.

While others pointed the finger of suspicion at Goodly and Grave, the Penny steadfastly supported them. Our intrepid reporter Slimeous Osburn was invited to Grave Hall to join in the celebrations of Goodly and Grave's success. As usual, the friendly banter between Slimeous and our two heroes flowed as freely as the champagne, with Lord Grave mischievously threatening to feed Slimeous to the lions in his wildlife park.

Dear Lucy,

We read in the Penny about the death of Mrs Charm, which we are very shocked and saddened at. But we are also very proud that you played a part in catching her murderer.

As for us, we are very well and enjoying the Casino di Venezia very much. We had a very strange experience, though! We both fell asleep at our hotel and didn't wake up for two whole days. We think it might have been a combination of the Venice air and too much gambling.

Now that we have made a comfortable amount of money we have decided to come home and begin a new life. We have decided against rebuilding Leafy Ridge. Instead, we are going to buy the Charm Inn with our winnings and turn it into a casino!

We hope to see you soon, darling girl.

Your ever loving parents

x

CHAPTER TWENTY-TWO

A PACT OR TWO

Lucy gasped at the monster in front of her. It was tall and thin with a massive shiny black head, like some kind of hideous overgrown insect. Raising her hand, not to ward off the monster, but to pat her own hair, Lucy watched as the mirror distorted the reflection of her fingers to round blobs of flesh. Smell, who was standing next to her, sniffed at his elongated mirror-self and then pretended to snarl.

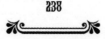

"Look at the size of them fangs!" he said.

Lord Grave, Lady Sibyl and Lord Percy were grouped around a different mirror, which gave their reflections animal heads. Lord Grave was a stag, Lady Sibyl a horse and Lord Percy an eagle. Even Bathsheba was transformed, her reflection bearing the head of a mouse. Beguildy Beguildy was gazing awestruck at an image of himself as a king sitting on a golden throne, while Prudence laughed gaily into a mirror, which showed her carrying her severed head under her arm. As for Bertie, he was busy going from one mirror to the next, examining each closely from every possible angle. He was convinced he could find an explanation other than magic for how they worked, even though Lord Grave had told him they were enchanted.

There was one other rather excited individual in the O'Brien's Midnight Circus Hall of Mirrors. The golem Jerome Wormwood had created. It was currently gawping at itself transformed into a young and handsome man in one of the magical mirrors. After the events in St Olaf's graveyard, MAAM had

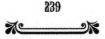

been left with the tricky question of what to do with the golem. It would have been usual to destroy such a monster, but Lucy had felt very uncomfortable with that idea. She'd argued that the golem had demonstrated some very human characteristics in its appreciation of music and in the way it had resisted the demands of both Wormwood and Thorne. After much deliberation and consultation with experts, Lord Grave had eventually decided to give the golem a chance. It was now undergoing rigorous training to curb any violent tendencies as well as regular manicures and pedicures to blunt its nails.

Roland Mole was of course furious not to be able to have his Emerald Eye back, but Lord Grave said it would be unethical to remove one of the golem's eyes. As for the other Emerald Eye, strictly speaking that belonged to Mortimer Thorne who had given it to Dolores Charm for safekeeping when he went to prison. But as he had stolen it off someone else somewhere along the line, it seemed fair for the golem to hang on to it.

The trip to O'Brien's Midnight Circus was the

golem's first social engagement. Lord Grave had been a little surprised and initially reluctant when Diamond O'Brien had invited him and the rest of MAAM to join her for afternoon tea at her circus. However, she had explained that, following the terrible events of the last few days and the death of two magicians, she felt the magical community needed to come together. Lord Grave had to agree that she had a point and so accepted the invitation.

When everyone had finished admiring their reflections, they made their way to Diamond's caravan, where a table was laid, loaded with a variety of food for the guests to choose from. Lucy was about to select a particularly delicious-looking jam and cream bun when her hand collided with Beguildy Beguildy's. They both hesitated.

"You take it," Lucy said.

Instead of politely declining, Beguildy showed no hesitation in swiping the bun. Lucy sighed and selected an equally delicious-looking slice of sponge cake. She knew this was her chance. Beguildy was as annoying as ever, but she did have something to thank him for. She'd been avoiding speaking to him about it until now, but as this seemed to be an afternoon of reconciliation, she had decided she should give it a try if the opportunity arose.

It took her a couple of attempts to get the words out, but she eventually said, "I've never properly thanked you. Lord Grave told me you were the one who guessed Rivers, I mean Wormwood, had taken me away. If you and the rest of MAAM hadn't turned up when you did, it could have all got very awkward for me."

There had been a lot of clearing up to do in the aftermath of the drama at St Olaf's. Memories had been tweaked (including those of her parents, whom Lucy had then shortcut back to Venice), and Mortimer Thorne rearrested. As for Jerome Wormwood, he had realised his dearest wish and was now reunited with his beloved master. The two men were sharing a cell in Millbank Prison and, according to reports, did not get along very well at all.

"You're welcome," Beguildy said in a slightly strangled voice. He took a large bite of cake.

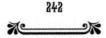

"How did you guess that Rivers was Jerome Wormwood?" Lucy asked. Of course, Lord Grave had already told her this, but she wanted to keep the conversation going.

Beguildy chewed and swallowed. "I'd been suspicious of him for a while. He kept pumping me for information. And he always seemed to be loitering around doors every time there were discussions of any importance. So when you both vanished, I was certain that he was up to something bad. We searched his room. Found a bottle of black hair dye and a bundle of letters from Diamond O'Brien addressed to Jerome Wormwood as well as drawings of Millbank Prison."

"You were cleverer than me," Lucy said. "I trusted him completely until the very end."

"While you suspected *me* of being Wormwood," Beguildy said, grinning slyly.

Lucy's face grew warm. "Lord Grave shouldn't have told you about that! I am sorry. You might be irritating, but you're not evil. Maybe we'll never be best friends, but we do need to work together, so . . ." Lucy stuck her hand out.

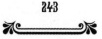

Beguildy stared at Lucy's hand as though it was something slightly unsavoury, but then he relented and the two of them shook hands, albeit very briefly. As they did so, Lucy became aware that the whole caravan was listening intently to her and Beguildy's exchange. They all began to applaud.

"Hooray!" Prudence said.

"Don't get over-excited, Prue," Beguildy said acidly.

"I love an 'appy ending," Smell said, dabbing at his eye with his paw. "Now, is there any more of them fish-paste sandwiches, Diamond?"

THE END

Acknowledgements

Huge thanks to . . .

My agent, Kate Shaw, for being fabulous and wise, as always. My brilliant editor, Harriet Wilson, for tirelessly helping me transform my rambling ideas into coherence. All the rest of the team at HarperCollins *Children's Books*, particularly Elisabetta Barbazza for her gorgeous design. Becka Moor for her wonderful illustrations, which capture the story so beautifully. My sister, Nikki Malcolm, along with Claire Lawton, Amanda Harries and the Wards for cheerleading *Goodly and Grave*. Team Escape – Liz Card, James MacDougall and Heather White, who saved my sanity during difficult times. And, above all, thanks to my husband for putting up with me being completely immersed in another world for so much of the time, and for soothing my irrational worries.

WHAT'S HAPPENING NEXT AT GRAVE HALL?

FIND OUT IN THE NEXT

GOODLY AND GRAVE

ADVENTURE!

COMING SOON!

DON'T MISS THE FIRST ADVENTURE!

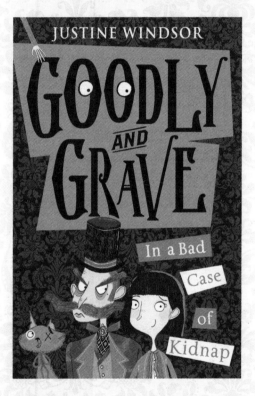

JUSTINE WINDSOR

GOODLY AND GRAVE

In a Bad Case of Kidnap

Could the mystery of the missing children
be linked to the strange goings-on at Grave Hall?
Lucy is determined to find out ...